A KISS FROM A
FAERIE KING

KISS FROM A MONSTER SERIES
BOOK 4

CHARLOTTE SWAN

1

LAURELLE

This dress was made to torture its wearer.

There is no other explanation for its construction. If it was not built for punishment, the designer definitely had a twisted sense of humor. Every breath pushes my ribs painfully against the unyielding fabric. My head pounds from the lack of breath. It's as if this *thing* is drowning me on dry land.

It's a slow, tortuous death, and yet it pales in comparison to what awaits me at the end of this journey.

Despite my protests, my mother had deemed my discomfort wholly necessary given who was about to receive me. It eradicates the curves my mother considers unbecoming of a respectable young woman, as if my maturing was a personal affront to her constitution.

The purple fabric of the gown is stiff and far too thick for this weather. The hot sun leaks through the carriage windows as we roll along. Sweat slips down my neck, and I know the curls framing my face that my mother had so carefully placed are damp and rapidly losing their perfect coils.

She would be most displeased if she saw the state of me.

As would my father, though nothing seems to please him these days beyond an elevation in status. Apparently, the payment for this elevation comes in the form of this satin prison and a few thousand gold coins.

I swallow. The high neck of my gown obstructs even that movement. I go to lift my hair from my neck, but the sleeves of my gown won't allow my arms to rise higher than my chest.

This journey to the palace will be unbearably long. Even my companion doesn't know where to look or what to do. I can't say I blame Caryssa. If my upbringing was hard, hers was unbearable, especially with a brother like hers.

Her brother...my intended.

Our engagement will not be finalized until I am received at court and my father ships over the dowry owed to my soon-to-be husband. What my father lacks in station, he makes up for in wealth. Our deficiency of connection has always been a thorn in his side.

It was clear to me from an early age that he would earn a title by any means necessary. His children were mere pawns in his game. My siblings had been quite a bit older than me and were already married off to various noblemen by the time I was ten.

Unluckily for me, I had the rare opportunity of marrying a prince.

My mother falling pregnant a few years after the prince's birth was no coincidence. Even if she had been older—the risks higher—none of it mattered so long as my father had a chance at infiltrating royalty. For all of her faults, my mother is a pawn in all of this as well.

I should be happy to have a title and security within my husband's household, but I cannot find it within myself to do anything but sit in quiet contemplation. To be the meek and silent girl my parents cultivated as soon as I was young enough to be paraded in front of suitors. My dreams and desires are worthless in the face of my father's ambitions.

Try as I might, my heart still holds on to them, even as every moment spent in this carriage leads me closer to a fate not of my choosing.

I glance out the window as we continue along the Lord's Road. When Princess Caryssa came to collect me, we had shopped in town. I had been informed of Prince Carysen's fondness for the color red. My mother would be proud of how well I kept my composure while my stomach flipped over the idea of dressing for his *pleasure*.

Our royal escorts advised us we needed to set off before sundown. Silently, I watched as they packed the carriage full of red fabric and gowns quickly tailored to my size. If only this carriage could've caught on fire before we climbed inside. I'd rather them be turned to ash than wear them for Prince Carysen.

Caryssa is young, barely older than sixteen, and of a nervous disposition. Even as we sit in silence, I dare a glance over to her and watch her wring her hands for the hundredth time.

Between her silence and this dress, I don't know what's making me more uncomfortable.

I can bear it no longer and decide to break the quiet myself.

"Have you been presented at court yet, princess? Your sixteenth name day was only a few months ago?" I ask. Caryssa's eyes dart up to meet mine. They are a lovely shade of blue. Her hair is just a few shades too dark to be considered blonde, as it sparkles in the dim light of the carriage.

"I—yes, my lady. I was presented when I was fourteen," she says softly.

"That's quite young." Her chin dips, and she shifts uncomfortably. Is her blue gown made of the same horrendous material as mine? I can only imagine it is. "Was it your mother's idea?"

She shakes her head.

"My father's. He feels it's best I secure a betrothal now before I get any aspirations of my own." The princess blanches at her own words, her light eyes widening as they meet mine. My stomach sinks as my suspicions are confirmed. Whatever scrupulous rules I was under in my family's home will undoubtedly follow me into my marriage.

"I understand, princess. Our fathers seem quite similar."

"My apologies, my lady. I shouldn't have spoken out of turn like that," Caryssa says, her face turning even paler. "I would never want to speak of my father that way. He is a good man—complicated in the way all powerful men are."

I nod my head, my gaze staying on her face. She looks so young. I'm nearly ten years her senior. Something in me wants to protect her from the dangers of the world. I also want to ask my own mother if I looked that young when she brought me to court for the first time as well.

Caryssa begins wringing her hands again. I dip my chin to try and capture her eye.

"Princess, you may call me Laurelle. We are to be sisters, are we not?"

"Laurelle," she says, testing my name on her tongue. "That's pretty. Call me Caryssa, though it's a name nowhere near as lovely."

"What would you want it to be?" I ask.

"Want what to be?" She arches a golden brow at me.

"Your name. If you could pick any in the world, what would it be?"

The princess scrunches her nose, deep in thought. For a moment, we seem like two ordinary girls. Sisters even despite looking nothing alike. I could befriend her, help her break free of this cycle that not even my own dreaming could save me from.

Caryssa's eyes pop open, and a smile graces her lips.

"I think I would like it to be—"

The carriage jerks to a halt, and we nearly fall off the benches. The sudden jarring movement causes my lacing to squeeze my ribs even tighter. This thing is unbearable. If I had the power to do anything in the world, I'd rip this dress off and never wear another corset again. Or another pair of stiff shoes. Every day, I would wear thin cotton and walk barefoot through the world.

I'm sure my mother's neck felt a chill by merely thinking that.

Ignoring my throbbing sides, I reach out and touch Caryssa's shoulder.

"Are you alright?"

"Fine," she says, though I notice her wincing too.

"Apologizes, Your Majesty," comes a voice through the carriage window. Glancing over, I see the silver top of a guard's helmet. "The storm last night upended a tree in our path. The road is blocked, but there's a shortcut through *The Woods*. We'll be back on our path in no time."

My heart pounds in my chest at the mention of them.

"*The Woods*?" Caryssa's wary voice echoes my own sentiments. Growing up this close to them, the stories were told throughout my village. Many said they were simple tales to scare misbehaving children, but I'm not sure. There is an eeriness to them, as if something or someone unsavory is lurking in the tree-line.

"We will be quick, princess," the guard assures her. "The

sun isn't setting for at least another hour. That's more than enough time to return to the Lord's Road."

"Of course," Caryssa agrees, though her face is still sallow. "Thank you."

The guard stomps off, and it's only a few more moments before we begin rolling again. Caryssa still looks unsure, especially as the terrain turns uneven. The jostling of our carriage is only exacerbating the pain from my corset.

"Tell me about your brother," I say, trying to distract the both of us from the discomfort.

"Oh," Caryssa whispers. "He's—well, he's um…"

Her eyes drift around the carriage. Again, her hesitation only serves to make my discomfort grow. I knew what I was being sent off to do. With my marriage to Prince Carysen, I'll be a princess. In exchange for my hand and a very large sum of gold, my father will become a duke. I had been less than happy when my father told me of this betrothal.

Barely managing to keep it together long enough to be excused, I locked myself in my room and sobbed quietly, hiding the evidence before word of my response reached my mother's ears. They wanted me to be grateful. Grateful that I was marrying a man who made my skin crawl. Who I had met one time and who had been obscenely drunk. Who's eyes and hands wandered. Who cornered me during the evening, and if we had not been interrupted by servants, I shudder to think what would've happened.

Grateful to be marrying a man who has a reputation for *misplacing* his brides-to-be.

If the rumors are true, I'm his tenth intended in under two years. *Worthless gossip*, my mother had called the rumors when I questioned how he was available once more for marriage. We heard he was marrying another princess from a faraway kingdom. Only for her to turn up missing a few days after her arrival.

I hope for my sake they are only rumors. Would death be better than a marriage to that beast? Is this what my life has become? When I was younger, I had so many dreams and desires. I had plans for my future. Wants and hopes, and now I'm being driven headlong into my grave.

When I was young, I fantasized about my marriage. It was usually to a faceless hero, a knight who had saved me from a dragon, or a handsome king who saved me from my arithmetic lessons. When I was older, my desires matured with my body. A few of our cooks passed around short novels filled with the most salacious passages. My mother confiscated it and fired them all, but not before I could steal a few sections of the book.

I read the pages over and over until they disintegrated in my hands. Those wanton activities intrigued me because they were in such sharp contrast to my cold, demure life. I dreamed that my marriage bed was the time I could lie in a man's embrace and bring my pleasure-soaked fantasies to life.

To have my hero tame the ache between my legs formed by those smut-filled stories.

The thought of sharing a bed with Prince Carysen has my stomach cramping. I can't go through with this, but what choice do I have? I can't return home. I have no money of my own. Where would I go?

A part of me says it doesn't matter; anywhere is better than arriving at the palace. As my eyes glance out the carriage window, my hopes of escape are dashed even further. The foliage around us is thick. Even if I managed to escape the carriage, how would I navigate this harsh terrain? Especially in a dress this restrictive.

I huff a humorless laugh. Caryssa's eyes land on my face before quickly glancing away. Is this my life now? Uncomfortable silences and unfulfilling marriage. Is a title worth giving up on everything I ever wanted for myself?

Is it worth giving up the chance of finding true love?

"Be honest with me," I say, finding Caryssa's eye again. "I will find out the truth soon enough. What is your brother really like? Please, Caryssa, tell me."

The princess bites her lip and glances through the window. Her voice is low when she speaks as if someone is just outside the carriage listening.

"He's cruel, Laurelle. Very, *very* cruel. My father was thrilled when he made that deal with yours. Our money...is gone. The royal banks are empty. The people have already begun to starve, and we are surely next. Your father offered a much-needed solution. Beyond that, my brother needs to be married off...his reputation...I mean, you must've heard the stories."

My palms begin to sweat.

"Are the stories true, Caryssa?" I ask. Her paling face is all the answer I need.

"They didn't run away. My brother can be rough, and the things I've seen him do..."

She trails off, and my ears begin to ring. I fall back against the bench seat. The carriage tilts around me, and I can't suck down enough air. My bones feel like metal, weighing me down.

How could my parents give me to a man like that? The answer is painfully simple. I've never been more than an opportunity. I'll die for my father's ambition. Will that make it worth it to him?

"What do I do, Caryssa?" I ask, my voice barely above a whisper. Moisture stings my eyes, but I refuse to cry. I will not be scared. Carysen doesn't deserve my fear or my tears.

"I—" Caryssa begins before a loud crash rips through the carriage's interior.

The carriage jerks and twists, dumping Caryssa and me to the floor. The impact rattles my ribcage and steals my breath. Caryssa lands on top of me, our heads knocking together. We both grunt in pain. The carriage lurches again, and we are jolted once more.

"Fuck!" someone shouts from outside.

"Grab hold of it!"

"Princess, are you hurt?"

The carriage comes to a harsh stop before the door is yanked open, and two guards reach in to pull us out. I wobble on my feet, touching the tender spot where our heads smacked together. My fingers come away clean. Caryssa comes stumbling out and is a bit worse for wear.

Her palm is cut, and crimson blood seeps into the sleeve of her gown.

I blink my eyes and take in the sight of the carriage. It's completely flipped onto its side. The cause of the accident lies still spinning a few feet away. The front right wheel has completely snapped off. The spindles are in splinters, and the axle is ripped off.

"What happened?" I ask the nearest guard. He shakes his head, his helmet obscuring his features.

"We're not sure. It was rolling just fine until...it wasn't. As if some unseen force just broke the wheel off."

"It's this place. It's cursed," Caryssa whispers, coming to my side. I look down at her and gently take her uninjured hand.

"Are you hurt beyond your palm?" I ask. She shakes her head.

"What about you?"

"I'm fine. Let's get you cleaned up."

"Stay close," the guard next to me says. "We'll work fast to fix this while we still have the light. However, we don't know what prowls these woods, and the king will have our heads if you both aren't returned."

I gulp but nod as I lead Caryssa towards the back of the carriage.

The guards crowd around the broken wheel, leaving us unwatched—the hairs on the back of my neck rise. *The Woods* are unsettling. It feels like a million eyes watch me as I tear a strip of fabric from my dress and bind Caryssa's hand. She hisses slightly before biting her lip in discomfort. Her light eyes dart towards the guards.

Even at a distance, I can hear them grunt and curse. There's no way this wheel will get fixed anytime soon, and I don't feel like spending a night in these woods.

"Well, it seems like fate is granting us a bit more time together before we return to the palace," I say, giving her a soft smile. Her eyes are still on the guards as she chews her bottom lip. "Are you sure you aren't hurt worse?"

I place my hand on her forehead and try not to recoil. She's as cold as ice.

"Caryssa, you're freezing. Here—"

"Laurelle," she whispers, capturing my hand. "You need to run."

Her words cause my own blood to ice over.

"What?" I ask, glancing at the guards, who are still gathering around the wheel.

"You can't go to the castle. He'll kill you."

"Caryssa, where would I go? I have a duty to—"

"A duty to nothing," Caryssa spits. Her eyes were like blue fire, a fury I'd never seen before kindling them. "You are kind and caring. I was too young or afraid to save the others, but I can't let their fate befall you. Run, run now."

My hands shake as her words wash over me.

"Here." Caryssa is already moving and leaving me no time to consider her words.

She shoves a small coin purse into my hand. My fingers curl around it.

"There's a town a few miles down the Lord's Road before we pulled off. A merchant is there who can give you passage somewhere else—somewhere safe. I've been in contact with him myself. For when the time comes where...I need to make my escape."

"Caryssa." My hand curls around hers. A girl as young as her shouldn't have these worries. "Come with me. I can't leave you behind."

She shakes her head.

"I'd only slow you down. Don't worry about me, but go now. Before the sun fully sets and you lose the path back towards the road."

I grip her hand again, giving it a gentle squeeze.

"Thank you, Caryssa. Truly."

I lift up my skirt and slip off my uncomfortable slippers. My toes dig into the soft grass of the forest. With a harsh jerk, I rip my gown off before loosening the laces of my corset. I suck down my first mouthful of air, savoring the crispness of it. Caryssa's eyes are round as she watches me.

"I can't run in that thing."

Caryssa nods and nudges my shoulder.

"Go, I'll distract them."

"How?" I ask. She bends down, picks up one of my slippers, and holds it towards me.

"Hit me with this."

"What?" I whisper, my mouth falling open.

"Just hit me with it and run. I'll do the rest." I grip the silken slipper in my hand. I cringe as I raise my arm above my head.

"Sorry," I whisper before bringing the slipper down on the side of her head.

Before the slipper hits the ground, I'm already running. I hear Caryssa's scream and rush towards the guards. My braided hair whips in the wind as I pump my legs. I haven't run in a long time, and it's showing as I'm quickly winded.

"Hey! Grab her. Get back here!"

"Lady Laurelle, come back!"

The guards shout after me, but my steps don't slow. *The Woods* swallow me up the deeper into them I get. I don't know how far away the road is or if I'm even traveling in the right direction, but I don't stop. My corset still constricts me, so I rip the laces off and let the damn thing fall behind me, never slowing my steps.

Metal clanks behind me as I careen sharply to the right.

"Stop running!" a voice calls from a few feet back.

My legs burn, and my feet are cut on sharp sticks. The cold air licks over my heated skin, and sweat pools along my spine. I take another sharp right and fling myself behind a large boulder.

Panting, I slap a hand over my mouth to silence my breaths. Metal footsteps continue past me as I sit still in the fading light. My thick shift is a mess. Shredded along the hem and the sleeves. I gently peel it away as I survey the damage to my feet and legs.

The cuts aren't deep, but I must clean them before they fester. I sit in the dark until I hear an owl hooting overhead. The sun has fully set. The large, pale moon illuminates the forest. The stillness of it all is unsettling. No animals beyond the owl rattle the branches or bushes around me. I would think I was if it wasn't for the feeling of being watched.

I don't know how long I sit in the dark, but I know it's not wise to linger. I need to make it to that village. The guards have missed me for now, but they could return at any moment.

Limping forward, I continue on the dimly lit path. The night air is cold, and I begin to shiver, remembering that I am half-naked. It takes only a few minutes of aimlessly walking before I realize I'm truly lost. The trees I'm passing seem like ones I've already walked by.

My shoulders slump. This is my first taste of freedom, and I will perish in *The Woods* before getting to fully enjoy it. The grass turns damp beneath my feet as I continue forward.

A breeze blows my curls into my eyes. First, it's gentle, then more forceful. I let it guide me. It's as if *The Woods* are taking me somewhere, and I can only hope it's a way out—my heart lodges in my throat as my eyes adjust to the scene before me.

The tree line is thinning, and there is a clearing up ahead. My steps speed up. Have I reached the forest edge? Crossing through the tree line, I let out a groan. It's just a meadow with dark trees surrounding it on all sides. The moon shines overhead and illuminates the open space. This isn't an ideal place to be.

If the guards come upon me, there's nowhere to hide. I go to turn and head back the way I came when something stops me. Slowly, I twist back around and blink my eyes to focus them. My feet move of their own accord as I take in the sight.

What I'm seeing doesn't seem real. It looks as if it's from another world.

A single flower sits in the center of the clearing. The thick blue petals glow softly, already covered in a glistening dew. It's as if it's made from crystals and sapphires the way it sparkles in the moonlight. It's a siren's song, luring me in. The bright petals are in three full layers, surrounding a bright-white center.

It seems to pulse, and as I kneel before it. The bloom casts my skin in a blue glow.

I'm transfixed, and even as the brightness burns my eyes. I wipe the tears sliding from my eyes as my hand extends towards it. Tracing one large petal with my fingertip, I shudder at the softness of it. What's happening to me? Have I lost my mind in these woods? Did I hit my head in the carriage crash, and now I'm hallucinating?

Whatever is happening to me, I feel like a bug caught in a spider's web. The pain in my legs and the fear of being captured by royal guards fade from my mind. All there is is this flower. My fingers trace along the velvet stem.

I want it—more than I've ever wanted anything. Something must've happened to me during the crash. Nothing makes sense, but the only thing I care about is having this flower. I shouldn't pluck it. My intuition tells me it would be wrong, but I can't help it.

I need it, I need it, I need it.

"I'm sorry," I whisper toward the flower. It's too pretty to be plucked, but I'm selfish. I want to keep its beauty all to myself. My hand grips the stem as I yank it from the ground. Its roots seem impossibly long, as if growing here for centuries. I pull it towards me, enjoying its sweet scent... before my eyes widen as the petals atrophy. They turn dull and brown before curling in on themselves. It's only another moment before they turn into a cloud of dust that blows away in the night air.

"No!" I shout, my heart crumbling along with the bloom. *What have I just done? Why would I do that?*

I don't get to answer those questions as the ground below me shakes. The solid soil beneath my knees breaks away and disintegrates just as the flower's petals did. My scream is swallowed up by the dark abyss I'm sent tumbling down into.

2

EMRYS

My subjects could try the patience of the most even-tempered king.

The Great Oak knew in all its infinite wisdom that only a creature as strong-willed as myself could keep them in line. My power contains them in our realm far beneath the human world. Far away from *The Woods* our beloved oak tree sprouted from below. Its gnarled branches reached through the soil to separate our two worlds. It wasn't long before it became teaming with creatures from all manner of ilk. Flocking towards its ancient magic, they find their home amongst the dense foliage.

Deep beneath the ground, *The Great Oak's* roots grow strong and feed off the magic from our realm. Whether the magic existed because of the oak tree or the oak tree exists because of magic is one of our greatest mysteries. Regardless, I've always been its keeper. My reign has been from the beginning and will continue until the end.

As of late, it's been boringly tedious, as no one makes a fuss anymore.

There were centuries where I could hardly keep the

humans and other creatures from falling into my kingdom at an exorbitant rate. I had to put safeguards in place to keep them at bay, and they have worked, unfortunately, for my restless spirit. Now, I only have a few lost humans or a misbehaving sprite to entertain me. The creatures of the above world have decided to rule over their sections of *The Woods* and don't care to venture too close to mine.

Leaving me to toil away in my underground realm, the guard of the unchanging great tree, of the everlasting oak spirit...that is, until a few decades ago.

When *The Great Oak* lost its first leaf.

The sprites came to me, horror on their little glowing faces. Even the faeries—a naturally mischievous bunch— had looked solemn. Their dark eyes and two-foot-tall bodies were tense with unease.

Indeed, dread is what I felt watching that first golden leaf fall—floating on a gentle breeze until it landed softly on the damp grass. Shrieks rang out as it browned and curled before turning to ash in the wind.

The pain came next. A deep ache rattled my soul and caused me to double over. My pain was linked to it as its guardian. If I wanted to save myself, then I had to save it.

I knew the solution before the sprites flew to my ears to whisper it to me. I've always known what obligation I must fulfill, but even so, these meddlesome creatures don't give anyone, least of all me, their king, a moment's reprieve.

Even now, as I sit, the twilight setting in and coating our meadow in rich blue hues, their voices plague my ears. The three sisters, Puddle, Pond, and Port, are the most staunch weavers of this tale.

"This kingdom is sick," says Puddle.

"Sicker than sick," agrees Pond.

"Without a queen," Port rasps in my ear, "the plants won't grow."

I wave my clawed hand, scattering their plump, pink forms. Their clear wings sparkle as they dodge my movement. Their skin glows brighter, a glimpse at their dismay.

"That one didn't rhyme," I remark, scratching the base of my crown. It's a permanent fixture I was born with. Two mighty branches sprout from my forehead, their limbs reaching toward each other like interlocking fingers. Some days, especially recently, make it feel heavier than ever.

The sisters are right. Poor rhyming skills aside, the sentiment rings true. *The Great Oak* is dying. Countless leaves have been lost since the first one broke free. Each one wracks my body with excruciating pain. When it finally goes rotten, will I decay along with it? Each morning, I check for a decline in my outward health: a rotting tooth, a missing finger, or an eye turning milky and unseeing. Nothing has happened, but I have the distinct impression something will soon if I don't act.

"Plant the seed," the three sisters whisper. "Pull the weeds."

Their squeaky voices chant the saying in unison over and over. I bare my teeth at them, but they merely float to my shoulders. Weaving themselves in between the strands of my white hair, I can never stay mad at the sisters for too long. With a deep sigh, I rub the base of my crown once more.

"What would you have me do?" Their pink bodies zip in front of my nose. "To complete the ritual, I must mate in the heart of *The Great Oak*."

That is what legend says will save us all. If ever the power of the tree should wane, an offering of body and spirit made inside its heart will reignite it. Magic is created when two souls become one during the intimate act. It's primal magic—the type of magic that may have created *The Great Oak* in the first place.

It seems like a simple enough ritual to complete- except for one key component that's been missing these past centuries.

"I don't see you volunteering to complete it with me."

I raise a brow as the sisters burn into a hot magenta. Their wings flap quickly as the three of them fly in a circle.

"Oh no," sighs Pond.

"Not us," sings Puddle.

"Never, ever," cries Port.

"Don't act modest. I've seen what you three lustful creatures get up to. Together...and apart."

The sprites are as wanton as anything. I can hardly judge them. When you are nearly a millennia old, the list of things you haven't done is much shorter than the inverse. Still, the sisters are right. It can't be either of them, as I have no doubt they are about to remind me.

"Must be a human," chimes Pond.

"That's the only way," chuckles Puddle.

"Find one now," chirps Port.

I lift my hand towards the meadow around us.

A few unlucky humans mill about down here. The punishment for breaking into my realm is an eternity of servitude. Not that any of them seem to mind it. They're drunk on pleasure and an odious amount of faerie wine. I watch one human woman pass. Her eyes glazed over and heavy-lidded. She's been here for almost a century. Her bare feet snag in the damp grass as she's led by the sleeves of her sheer dress towards one of the many alcoves.

A debauched scene of her and some of my faeries will ensue shortly. The meadow does that to everyone. Wildflowers weave together in a mass of colors and fragrances while each is laced with magic to lower your inhibitions and heat your blood. A novelty I enjoyed for many centuries that I now find no longer holds much appeal.

My heart longs for more—a meeting and binding of my soul with another's. Part of that desire stems from my guardianship of *The Great Oak* and a need to complete the prophecy. However, I felt this restlessness within me before the first leaf fell. An unease that no amount of faerie wine and naked flesh could solve.

Despite the confusion within myself, one thing is clear: the human I need to complete the ritual is not currently in my service. It's been a few months since the last one slipped through. My faeries and sprites quickly sank their claws into them before I even got the chance to consider them as a partner in this ritual.

A part of me knows that even if my faeries hadn't gotten to our last human first, they wouldn't have been the right choice. I will not take just anyone into *The Great Oak*. Whoever I choose to complete the ritual will be it for me. My mate, my queen...I would not sully *The Great Oak* with anyone less than that.

Sitting on my oak throne, a gnarled branch digs into my back as my crown tightens at the base. The wood of my throne feels weaker—hollow—indicating that I'm failing at the one role I was created for. Closing my eyes, I inhale deeply. The sweet and smoky scent of the meadow fills my lungs as my hair blows in a gentle breeze.

Great Oak, I pray silently, *hear me. Guide me and help me so that I can serve you. Bring me the one I need for the ritual before it is too late for us all.*

The wind shifts as the leaves above me rustle softly. I would take it as a sign that *The Great Oak* heard my plea, but this isn't the first time I've called and been ignored. If the human I need doesn't arrive soon, we may be doomed.

"Tick-Tock," says Pond.

"Tick-Tock," repeats Puddle.

"Time's almost up," declares Port.

Breathing deeply through my nose, I raise my hand to swat at the pestering sprites when my whole body goes rigid. It's faint—barely rising above the earthly scent of the meadow—but it's there. Sweet and warm and unlike anything I've smelt before. My mouth waters from just the barest hint of it as I rise from my throne on wobbly legs.

The three sisters notice the change in my demeanor, but before they can give another infernal rhyme, a shrill scream cuts through the tittering of the faerie gathering. I huff a breath as the faeries around me shiver and shake, their excitement palpable as they shriek in unison.

"Human!" they wail, buzzing on translucent wings towards our latest arrival.

My subjects swarm towards the clearing—where the veil between my realm and the human world is thinnest—and I am powerless but to follow them. Rubbing the base of my crown, my head feels twice as heavy as I remember I am king.

My curiosity is peaked but I will wait for them to return with our *guest*.

There are various entrances all over the human world above that allow them access to my realm. Most find themselves here by accident—a few hedonistic souls do, however, seek us out. Less so now, as I'm sure the tales of my realm have turned into foreboding myths and legends.

This particular entrance has entranced even the most cautious human.

Though, if they have ventured this far into *The Woods,*

aren't they looking for ruination somehow? Only a truly desperate soul would come this far, and the fate befalling them by plucking my flower is better than one at the hands of the other beasts who roam the world above.

My lips pull back at the thought of this being another fur trader. There's been an influx of them lately—greedy souls who don't make for fun playthings. Dreadfully dull—even for humans. Their profession of killing and skinning for coin does not mix well with our faerie wine. The dozen of them wandering the fields with their open mouths and milky eyes is a testament to that.

If nothing else, I hope this thief who tried to steal my blossom is at least pleasant to look at. Their scent alone is more intriguing than a dozen fur traders.

Shrieks and screams of delight echo around me. Even the damp grass of the meadow seems to lean towards our newest arrival. The trees that encase my meadow sway on a gentle breeze. A few glowing bugs weave between their strong trunks. This meadow—my realm—seems foreign, yet I know it to be as familiar as my hand.

Something cold skates down my spine. I glance behind me to see if it's one of my subjects, but only a gentle wind greets me. I'm not given long to ponder my unease as the wails of pleasure from my faeries get closer. The hum of their tiny wings echo through the tree line.

I hold my breath as they approach. My lips twitch, urging me to pull them back from my teeth. *No need to snarl at our guest*, I think. *Yet, at least.*

Branches snap as they pour through and into the meadow. My faeries' bodies glow as they fly around. They float through the grass, dance along the branches of the trees, and with all their force, yank whoever was unlucky enough to try and steal from me.

A decidedly feminine whimper has my ears perking up. My shoulders droop slightly as my subjects drag her into the clearing. She swats at them, but it's useless. My faeries cover her completely, and I can only make out her hand. Then, only a glimpse of her foot and a curling tendril of her dark hair.

This angers me more than her intrusion.

"Enough!" I command.

In an instant, my faeries stop their frenzy and retreat from the human. Settling their sparkling forms into the grass at her feet, casting her a dim glow. The moon overhead illuminates her enough. My heart pounds as I take her in. This is no intruder—no thief in need of punishment. She is a goddess who walks the world above. The sun cast in mortal flesh. The moon sculpted into a female form.

She's perfect. She's *mine*.

Her simple cotton shift does nothing for her. Even if it seems it was once good quality, it's been tattered and torn, leaving swaths of her golden brown skin exposed to the glowing light. Her legs and arms are slim, but I won't be satisfied until I can see, touch, and taste every inch of her skin. The graceful slope of her neck leads up to a delicately pointed chin. Full lips and cheeks are surrounded by thick, shining black curls. My claws itch to thread through them, to watch the coils slip between my fingers and reform into their magnificent shape.

Delicate dark brows arch over the most beautiful eyes I've ever seen—a warm brown with honey swirled into her irises framed by thick lashes. They stare at me in shock—in fear—and my stomach lurches. She shouldn't be anything less than happy and pleased in my presence. Even as she looks unsure, warmth pours from her and heats my blood clear across the meadow.

Her full lips parted with a gasp as she trembled slightly. The wind blows her tattered shift, carrying her delicious scent. My cock stirs in my thin pants, and my mouth waters. It's sweet, sweeter than honey, than the ripest fruit. Like sun-drenched wildflowers, her scent has me taking a dazed step towards her.

"Who are you?" Desire has turned my voice to gravel.

Her wonderful eyes shift away from me before returning, kindled by fire.

"Laurelle," she says, her voice making my knees buckle. "I was—I was just passing through."

My beauty—she dulls the meadow around her—blinks her eyes rapidly as if waking up from a dream. The wild-flowers are muted and lifeless in comparison to her. She is a true blossom, an indulgent temptation.

"Where am I?" Her voice is a mere whisper. "How did I—"

She swallows hard and takes a shaky step back. I go after her, itching to touch her, but I hold back. She's skittish now, and I won't scare her further. My eyes are the only thing that will give away my hunger for her.

"Laurelle." I savor her name on my tongue. "Did you try and steal from my meadow? Plucked a flower that did not belong to you?"

"I," she gasps, "I didn't mean to. I'm sorry. Please, just let me go. I swear—"

I lick over my sharp teeth, pulling my lips into a smile.

"Humans come into my realm," I state. "None of them get to leave. It's the price for trying to take from me."

Laurelle takes another shaky step back and looks down. Quickly, as if finally noticing her state of undress, she wraps her arms around herself. I can't manage to swallow down my snarl. She should never cover herself. I'll show her that she is a treasure to behold.

There is no shame in my realm.

A grazing of soft wings tickles my ear as the three sisters weave between my hair and longue along my crown. I'm too transfixed by Laurelle to swat at them.

"The human we need," says Pond.

"The human to feed," agrees Puddle.

"The human to seed," states Port.

My heart pounds as I take in their words. Never has another affected me like this. Sure, I've spent years, decades, centuries engaging in illicit trysts fueled by lust, maybe even strong affection. However, this is...something bigger—deeper. Laurelle is different, and I can only hope that, for once, *The Great Oak* has finally answered my prayers.

The three sisters fly away as I move closer to Laurelle. Her sweet scent invades my lungs and settles in my stomach. Her eyes remain fixed on the ground as she takes deep breaths. Her shoulders rise and fall rapidly as I approach.

I stop just before my body grazes hers. My claws move slowly before gripping her chin. Her skin is warm and soft as I gently lift her beautiful face towards me. Being this close to her makes breathing hard, but somehow, I manage.

"Forgive me, I haven't properly introduced myself." My grin is as wide as her eyes. "I am the faerie king Emrys, and you, my blossom, belong to me now."

My thumb brushes her bottom lip, and she whimpers. Leaning in closer, my lips are a breath away from her ear. My tongue longs to taste, but instead, I settle for using it to deliver a promise.

"*Forever*."

3

LAURELLE

I tremble in the faerie king's solid grip.

Standing this close to him, I'm acutely aware of the fact that his hands are tipped in black claws that could easily shred my throat. I'm out of my depth here. Part of me feels like I'm trapped in a dream. A horrible, unnatural dream. How had I gotten to this place? Had I truly tumbled through the ground into a portal and...ended up here?

Wherever here is.

A chill runs through me as I consider the very real possibility that one of the royal guards caught and killed me. Now, my soul is trapped with these creatures for the rest of eternity as punishment for defying my father's wishes.

The king's grip tightens ever so slightly, and I'm jolted back into reality and into the strange world I now find myself in. This is all real, too real. The meadow's grass is damp against my bare soles. The night air is perfumed with the wildflowers that cover the ground. The creature in front of me smells like soil and crisp air.

Nestled in his white hair sits a crown of gnarled

branches that sprout into deep green leaves. A seemingly uncomfortable accessory to highlight his importance. His skin is pale, milky green save for the dark ends of his fingers. His eyes are completely black and glossy. He doesn't so much as blink as he surveys me from head to toe. His gaze is hot and curious as it runs along my body.

I may not have died, but I most definitely hit my head because my body isn't reaching as it should. I should be clawing at his grip, fighting to escape his heated stare. Instead, my body feels...strange. Aware and warm and not entirely unpleasant.

This creature seems to know this as his lips twist into a smile, revealing two rows of sharp teeth.

We stare at each other momentarily. My breath hitches as he drops his hand from my face. His gaze lingers down my body, and I'm reminded that I'm practically naked in my thin shift. It's tattered and torn, exposing more of my body than I ever have, save for my lady's-in-waiting, who helped me bathe.

Instinctively, I wrap my arms around my chest. My captor only smiles wider.

"Pond, Puddle, Port!" he growls, his voice practically feral. I watch with wide eyes as three plump sprites break from the others and shimmer before me. They glow a deep red before tangling in the king's long hair.

"Yes?" they giggle in unison.

"Prepare our guest." His tongue licks over his teeth on the last word. "We will have a feast tonight to celebrate her arrival."

Before I can unstick my tongue, the three shimmering beings lounging on the king's shoulders fly towards me. The three sprites glimmer and shake until they transform with a gentle glow. They land at my feet, larger than before but barely over a foot tall. However, they pull me with the strength of full-grown men.

The whole meadow around me erupts in cheers as they drag me over the slippery meadow. Two of them pull me by each arm while the other yanks me by the tattered hem of my shift. My head whips back as I stare at the king. His dark eyes narrow as he licks over his sharp teeth, causing me to shiver.

What is going on? Where am I? What's happening?

Why couldn't I voice my protests? I suppose they don't matter. I'm stuck here despite...everything. How have I managed to escape one unfortunate fate only to end up trapped in another?

The evening breeze on my heated skin feels real. Once again assuaging the idea that this is some delirious dream I'm having. The grass squishing between my toes feels sticky and familiar. The hands of the faeries dragging me are small, but they pulse with life and warmth.

Again, my voice is trapped inside my throat as my three chaperones lead me toward an opening in one of the larger trees. Its branches are lined with rich green and gold leaves. It's larger than any tree I've ever seen, with the hollowed-out trunk being wide enough for three of me to fit through. Once we pass through the wooden arch, the breath is stolen from me, and my feet pause.

"Keep walking," one sprite chirps.

"No stopping," complains another.

"Time is ticking," states the last.

They murmur to each other in more riddles, but I am transfixed on the sight before me. We're inside the tree, yet we are in a palace. A grand one with an entryway and tile-lined floor. A sparkling chandelier hangs from above, illu-minated with golden candlelight. It is in the shape of overlapping branches, matching the crown around the king's head. This place appears to stretch far back—seemingly endless despite us being nestled inside a tree.

It makes no sense, yet nothing here seems to.

"Hurry, you're too important to delay."

Small hands yank me again and I follow. The air inside is crisp and fresh. The three of them pull me past different rooms. A few are bedrooms with their beds decorated with fluffy pillows and silks. We pass another set of doors that seems to lead to a kitchen. The scent of fresh bread and roasting meats makes my stomach growl.

"What is this place?"

My voice is rusty from disuse. It sounds foreign to my own ears.

"The king's palace, of course," the one holding my right arm says.

"Quickly, Puddle, in here. Time is ticking," the one holding my left arm whispers.

"Don't rush. She must be perfect, Pond," responds Puddle.

"She will be. Right, Port?" asks Puddle.

"She already is."

The three of them continue their chatting before yanking me into another room. My eyes adjust to the bright light. Candles cover every surface. The walls are painted gold, and it matches the metallic veining decorating the pale tiles on the floor. Along one side of the room are three massive wardrobes. I watch in shock as they fill with an array of items. Silks and fine linen dresses hang from the inside. There are fresh shifts to replace my tarnished one. I'm unfamiliar with an array of short, silk garments I see being hung next to the rest of the items. It takes me a moment to recognize them, and only because of those salacious novels I once read. Nightgowns, they were called. Short and in every color of silk imaginable.

My face warms as the three faeries pull me in front of a large mirror. I gasp at my reflection. The evening has taken a toll on me. There are a few faint scratches along my cheek. Dirt is smeared across my forehead and nose, and I know there's plenty stuck under my nails. My curls are limp as they cling to my neck. My hair is one big tangle, having come loose from its braid.

"Come sisters, let's get to work," says Port. "Puddle, fetch material for her dress. The green will make her eyes glow. Pond, tend to her cuts, and clean her. I'll handle her hair."

The three turn their full, unblinking attention on me before they break into a flurry of activity. Their glowing bodies sparkle in the candlelight. Pond appears in front of me with a pair of golden scissors. I jerk back as she glides the cool metal up my shift.

Port pushes my shoulders and forces me into a plush, white velvet chair.

"What are you—"

The question dies on my lips as Pond uses her wings to fly up and slice my shift clean up the middle. With a wave of her hand, my shift slips off my shoulders and pools on the chair around my hips. I yelp and try and cover my breasts, but that only makes the three faeries around me giggle.

"Stop this!" I shout. "You can't just cut my clothing off."

The three sprites stop their laughing, and their glow dims a little. They don't seem remorseful. No, they seem more *confused*.

"But," whispers Puddle, "it was filthy."

"You can't just strip me. Not without asking me first. Bring me a robe to cover myself," I order, trying to remember my old life. Nudity is immodest and not something to be so cavalier about. I'm sure these three sprites, dressed in a mere smattering of leaves, have no concept of shame.

"A robe?" Pond asks.

"Humans," Puddle huffs. "So fickle. Just like all the others."

"No," Port chimes, "she's different. Even if she can't see it yet."

A damp cloth appears in Pond's hand, and she buzzes on her wings towards my face. I wave my hand to stop her movements as she leans towards the marks on my cheek. A new feeling settles into my bones. Anger. How dare these creatures drag me into their debasement? I am not like them. I do not want to be special to them.

"Don't touch me. I demand you let me go at once."

I pray they can't hear my shaking voice. It's hard to be authoritative while sitting naked in a chair. My cheeks heat as I catch a glimpse of myself in the mirror.

"You're never leaving," states Pond.

"I'm not staying." I cross my arms over my chest, my face flaming even further. "Wherever it is that I am. I need to get back to my world."

"You are in the faerie kingdom. *The Great Oak* has sent you to us," chimes Puddle, who's half buried in fabric from the wardrobe. "You will bring back life to our realm."

My brows lower. *What does that mean?*

I must've voiced my confusion because Pond swiftly responds, "The king will choose you."

"You will serve him," adds Puddle, floating towards me with gossamer green fabric.

"He will serve us," finishes Port, producing a wide-tooth comb and slowly brushing through the ends of my hair.

Her skin glows a deep magenta at my tangles before she

produces a bowl of water and a thick jasmine-scented cream. Her small hands rake through my curls, saturating them until she easily glides the comb from bottom to top. It's not an unpleasant sensation. It reminds me of the handful of times my mother was ever gentle with me as a young girl.

Still, I can't let this pleasure distract me from what they've just said.

"Serve him? What does that mean?"

That sets the three sprites into a fit of giggles once more. Their laughter echoes around the room. Pond dabs a wet cloth on my cut cheek, and I gasp as the scratch heals instantly. She gently wipes behind my ears and along my neck. I jerk as she grazes under my breasts and down my legs. My face warms as the the three share a look with their wholly black eyes.

"An innocent, I can smell," sings Pond.

"The king will be pleased, I can tell," chuckles Port.

"We must hurry. No time to dwell," chastizes Puddle, who's finished with my hair. My curls are perfectly formed and glossy in the light. Carefully, she drapes a few dark tendrils along my temple before braiding a top section of hair back from my face.

"Can you three stop speaking in riddles and give me a full answer?" I ground out.

"No," they say in unison.

I roll my eyes as they continue working on me. They're stronger than they look, and I'm certain I couldn't fight them off. Besides, where would I even escape to? I fell through the ground. I'm sure there's no way back to the surface unless one of them helps me, and if they already believe I belong to their king...

My options for escape are slim, so I shall do what I have

always done and bide my time. When the opportunity to flee arises, I will take it. I have to. I can't stay here even if I have nowhere to return to.

Pond rubs her warm hand across my cheeks to add a bit of pink dust to them. Next, she uses the same hand across both my eyelids and lashes to darken them. Lastly, a dark-colored berry appears that she rubs across my lips, turning them into a deep red. This is no modest amount of make-up. My mother would be horrified at my wanton appearance.

When they slip the sheer gown over me, I know for certain that my mother would've keeled over at the sight.

The thin green fabric hugs my body, molding to each curve that was deemed unladylike even when I was still a girl. The fabric is thin enough to show everything from my hard nipples to the shadowy place between my thighs. The color warms the golden brown of my skin and makes my dark eyes shine.

My chest rises and falls as I take in my appearance. I look strange—like I belong in a place like this. I should feel ashamed or uncomfortable, but as my bare feet curl onto the cool tiles, I feel...free. The strict rules of society don't apply here, and for a fleeting moment, I let myself consider the life I'd have down here. Of course, there's always a possibility that their idea that my *service-to-the-king* will result in my beheading.

Though, judging by the hot stare the king looked me over with, I think he has another plan for my body rather than turning it into a corpse. What would that be like? To be owned by a creature like him? Would it be as freeing as I feel now?

The three sisters sigh and break me from that thought. I'm trapped here and need to figure out a way to escape.

Whatever the king's ownership of me entails, I am certain I do not wish to find out.

"She looks just right," Port states. "The king will be pleased with our work."

"I can't go out there like this." My protests sound half-hearted even to my own ears. "It's immodest—immoral. To show this much skin is unbecoming."

"Those words don't exist here," snaps Puddle. "Forget them, or you will be punished."

I swallow hard as they take my arms and skirt once more and pull me from the room. The palace around us passes in a golden blur. My feet feel the cool grass as we reemerge outside. The sun has set, and there is a chill to the floral-scented air. Glowing bugs and faeries weave between the thicket of trees. There is a hum of life as the large, pale moon hovers above, casting us all in its blue light.

How is the sky visible if we are underground?

The three of them lead me back towards the king's throne. Faeries and sprites of all shapes, sizes, and colors sip from golden goblets. They dance, their bodies shimmering and naked. Music floats through the air as a few engage in some sort of dance. It looks more like a mating ritual with their grinding bodies and wandering hands.

Do they expect me to allow the king to touch me in such a way?

My breath catches as I register more figures in the meadow's clearing. They're too big to be faeries or sprites. Their skin is too dull. Tucked amongst the creatures cele-brating are humans. Or at least the husks of some of them. Their hair is long and unkempt, as is their clothing. Their eyes are milky—clouded as they drink from their own goblets. Their mouths are red, like mine, but twisted into pleasured smiles.

Any thought that they could help me escape is quickly forgotten.

"That could've been you," whispers Puddle, who returns to her original small size and perches on my shoulder. "Still could be if you're not careful."

I suck in a breath as the other two sisters continue pulling me into the clearing. I try to delay as best I can, but it is of no use. My toes curl into the grass as we stop before the king. He sits shirtless. His pale chest is muscular, as are his arms. He's a large man—male? Whatever he is, his figure is most imposing.

His throne is carved into the base of a large oak tree. Hallowed out to accommodate his strong thighs that are barely contained in his dark linen pants. His black eyes miss nothing as they survey me from head to toe. My nipples harden further, and I wretch my arms free from the sisters to try and cover myself. A reflex I can't help.

The king growls, baring his sharp teeth, and I dip my head. My face heats, and shame curdles my stomach. Am I embarrassed of my body? Am I uncomfortable because that's how I feel or because I was taught to be?

The music around me stops, and my heart speeds up as I hear the creaking of wood followed by strong footsteps stomping towards me. The king's scent reaches my nose— dark and woodsy. It invades my mouth and chokes me, turning my skin warm and my lips dry.

His feet come into view. Before I can say anything, his strong hand wraps around my neck and jerks my face upwards. The touch doesn't hurt but leaves me in no doubt of his power. His thumb drags along the pulse at the side of my throat. My heart beats wildly as I meet his unrelenting stare.

At this angle, he's easily a foot taller than me. My neck

cranes all the way back to look up at him. His crown cast in moonlight makes him look even more dangerous. I should be immobile with fear. I most certainly shouldn't be overcome with this foreign yet not entirely unpleasant sensation. A warmth spreads from my stomach and into my lower extremities, causing them to prickle with awareness.

"Do not hide yourself from me," the king, Emrys, growls. His sharp teeth gnashing.

His power overwhelms me. My knees wobble, and shockingly, I want to obey him. Shame still holds me back, and for the first time in my life, I feel anger toward my parents for instilling it in me. I want to be wild and wanton in a way befitting of this place even if that thought is ridiculous.

I couldn't possibly stay here.

I swallow against his hold and nod my head. His lips tip as his hand lets go of my throat. Sharp claws skim over the exposed skin of my collarbone. I swallow down a yelp—a moan, really—before his hand encircles my arm.

"Come, you are my guest. Let me tend to you."

Gently, he leads me forward. I glance back at the three sisters, fluttering on their shimmering wings and nodding eagerly. Their color deepens before zooming away, presumably to engage in the festivities around us.

Emrys settles on his smooth, wooden throne, and before I can drop to the space next to him, he guides me towards his lap. I take a deep breath before perching on his thigh. A few thin layers of fabric separate our naked skin. A fact I'm distinctly aware of as I hold myself stiffly. The king only chuckles and curls a lock of my hair around one of his black-tipped claws.

"If you're good, I'll reward you," he states, dropping the

strand of my hair. "I'll show you all you can be in my realm if you let me."

I swallow against my dry throat. I have no idea what he means, and I don't think I'll be sticking around to find out. Despite my state of undress and my confusing feelings, I reach back into myself—into the training I've had as a child when it comes to royalty. In my experience, it's best to be seen and not heard. With that in mind, I sit silently on the king's lap as the warmth of his muscular leg seeps into me.

There's a comfort from him that has my posture relaxing. As the minutes or hours tick by, my shoulders begin to droop. His claws skimming up my back don't help my steely resolve as my body weakens in its rigid posture. My eyelids grow heavy as I watch the scene before me. The music plays with a renewed fever. The band of sprites and faeries bang away on small drums and their tiny hands pluck at harps and saw at a few wooden fiddles.

More wine flows as various berries and breads are passed around.

Suddenly, I'm overcome. Too tired to fight to resist the king's pull, I let my rigid posture go. The adrenaline from the fall—from being primped, pampered, and presented to this monstrous king—leaves me as I lean more fully into this male. To his credit, he doesn't touch me more than lightly on my back. It would be easy for him to take advantage of the situation, especially as sleep threatens, but something tells me I know he won't.

If that was his goal he could've easily done it by now. Besides, as my eyelids fully shut, I have no choice but to trust him. I let his warmth thaw my icy resolve and melt away the last of my self-preservation. With a deep breath, I inhale his scent as I tumble headlong into a new darkness filled with all-seeing dark eyes and razor-sharp smiles.

4

EMRYS

S he weighs nothing as she sleeps soundly against my chest.

The soft curls of her hair tickle my cheek as she shifts her position. The thin fabric of her dress renders her practically naked in my arms. Her chest rises and falls—the perfect swells of her breasts teasing the low neckline. She's lovely and warm.

Laurelle glows brighter than any star above.

As content as I am to watch her slumber—no doubt she's feeling the effects of all she's experienced this evening —I want to rouse her. I want to question her and hear her voice once more. I want to watch fire rage in her warm, brown eyes, and more than anything, I want to know what or who she was fleeing that sent her right into my trap.

Not that I'm complaining. I would've found her eventually somehow, but if she has enemies above, I need to know about them.

So I can eradicate them for her, of course.

Then there is the matter of her shyness. The three sisters had whispered in my ears after she fell asleep. They worried about her...*skittishness*. The shame she feels over being exposed. My teeth grind together as I remember her trying to cover her body from me. I will rid her of that shame—the word does not exist in my realm.

A few of my faeries and sprites fly up next to us. They come carrying overflowing goblets of sweet faerie wine and a variety of bread and cheeses atop golden serving platters. Settling the trays on a small table next to my throne, they quickly flutter away on their sparkling wings to rejoin the revelry happening around us. The air is thick with excitement and lust. The music filters through the trees, and the moonlight illuminates the night-blooming flowers all around us.

However, it all pales in comparison to the blossom in my arms.

Dear *Great Oak*, she is so gorgeous. In sleep, she is the picture of relaxation. Her golden brown cheeks are full and dusted with a smattering of freckles. I long to count and taste each one. Her dark lashes fan over them like delicate lace. Her nose is small and slightly upturned, dotted with more delicious freckles. Her mouth is slightly parted as she sleeps, inviting me in to taste her red lips. The make-up the three sisters put on her only enhances her beauty. When she was fresh-faced before me earlier, she was just as tempting.

I should let her rest, to not overwhelm her, but I am a weak king. I know it to be true when my finger lifts towards her cheek, and I gently trace her soft skin with the tip of my claw. She lets out a soft moan that has my cock jerking in my pants. I've been painfully hard all evening. Only she can take away this ache, but not yet. I must be patient, even if my finger continues its journey along the smooth contour of her jaw and down the delicate skin of her throat.

Her mouth opens wider on another moan, and I watch

in delight as her nipples harden against the front of her gown. Her sweet floral scent deepens, and I swallow down my own responding growl. Tracing my claw back up her face, I gently rub her lips with the pad of my thumb. Would she welcome my kiss?

Her eyes blink open, and I hold my breath. As if waking up from a pleasant dream, her eyelashes flutter as she yawns. In a flash, she goes from languid to rigid. Her small hand flattens against my shoulder and shoves me back. She's surprisingly strong for such a little thing.

Golden eyes blaze with newfound fury as she scurries from her place on my lap. She doesn't get far, but I do let her retreat further down my thigh.

"What are you doing?" she seethes, giving me another shove and fighting my grasp. I love her fire and will carefully stoke it for the rest of our life together.

She gives me another shove before freezing. Her face leeches of color as her mouthparts. My brows lower as her hands fold into her lap.

"I'm sorry," she whispers, staring at her clasped hands. I almost growl at her lack of eye contact. Her eyes should always be on me. "I shouldn't have—I mean, I didn't mean to—"

"Shh," I say, gently clasping her chin and forcing her stare back on me. Does she think I am upset by her resistance? If anything, I am hungrier for her after that show of strength.

Besides, it is me who should be apologizing, and I don't hesitate to do so.

"Relax, my little blossom. I am the one who's sorry. I moved too fast for you. I'll wait for you to be ready and welcoming to my touch."

Laurelle dips her chin, but her body remains stiff. As if remembering herself, her arms wrap around her chest, and she crosses her legs. A growl escapes me, and my claws sink into the arms of my throne.

"Why do you do that?" I ask through gritted teeth.

"Do what?" Her eyes shift away from me.

"Hide your beautiful body. Nudity is more than welcome here. It is encouraged."

I wave a clawed hand towards the clearing in front of us. Her cheeks color as she surveys the scene before us. Most of my faeries are naked in their small forms. Our human captives are as well. The sound of skin slapping together and high-pitched squeals of pleasure mix with the music. Pleasure is freely given and taken in my meadow. I want Laurelle to understand that. This will be her life now—with me—and the sooner she embraces it, the sooner we can begin partaking in it together.

"It's not," she pauses, her eyes returning back towards mine, "proper. A lady should be modest at all times. This type of behavior is unbecoming."

I bark a laugh. The words don't seem to be her own. They lack the conviction she's trying to convince herself they have.

My hand cups her petal-soft cheek, gently tracing her blush.

"You are no lady," I state.

Her head rears back as if she's been struck. Water pools at the bottom edge of her eye. She looks away, fighting to remove herself from my hold once more. The look of hurt splashing across her face has me reaching for her. Grasping her beautiful face once more, I let her see the earnestness of my words. I lay my desire for her bare in my gaze.

"You are no lady, Laurelle. You are much, *much* more than that. A gift—my gift. A goddess of old. My prisoner, one who's punishment is to be pleasured for eternity." She licks over her lips as I groan. "Not that that sounds like much of a punishment now, does it?"

Her lips curl into a smile before she shakes herself, her gaze guarded once more. We're making progress. I can see her fighting against her need for modesty. Her eyes drift back to the meadow before us.

"Will they be doing the...*pleasuring*?" She whispers the last word as if afraid someone may overhear.

I look over to the groups of faeries, sprites, and humans locked in *faerie-wine-fueled* couplings. I've had no qualms and have even been a willing participant in these wanton orgies in the past. However, Laurelle will not be partaking in them. I'd slaughter anyone else who dared touch her.

"No, my blossom, your sweetness is just for me."

Her body seems to relax, and I revel in her closeness once more. Who put these notions in her head? Who taught her to be afraid of her desires?

"You should feel no shame here. Lust and desire are natural feelings. There's nothing wrong about wanting to give yourself over to them," I tell her.

"I don't know," she says softly. "At first, I thought this place was a dream—that I'd wake up asleep in *The Woods*— but it all feels too real, and I don't...I don't know what to think now."

"It's best you forget whatever rules you lived by in the mortal realm. The sooner you understand that, the better." I renew my hold on her cheek. "I will not hurt you. No one here will."

"Because I'm special? The three sisters said I was meant

to serve you," she whispers, her eyes straying towards my mouth. Her body is warm and pilant, and I'd do anything to peel her out of her gown and ravish her in front of all those gathered here. I won't—I will wait.

She's too important. Too *mine*.

"Busy bodies, let's not think of that this evening." I lean towards the opposite side of my throne and grip one of the golden goblets. The faerie wine is dark in color, and golden flecks decorate the top. Its honey scent tempts my nose. "I want to know more about you."

"You do?" she asks.

"I want to know if you're willing to take the first step of letting go of who you were before. If you want to stay sheltered and shamed or if you wish to begin anew here, wild and wanton."

Taking a sip of the faerie wine, I let its hedonistic magic wash over me and overwhelm my senses. My desire for Laurelle was already strong, but the wine intensifies it further. I hold the goblet out towards her. The choice is hers. Whatever she chooses, I will accept.

I hold my breath as Laurelle licks over her lips. Her pupils dilate as she stares down at the wine. Slowly, she brings her delicate hand up to wrap around the base of the cup. Lifting it towards herself, I watch her take a deep breath.

Her eyes meet mine, and my blood grows molten.

"Wild," she answers softly.

Taking a small sip, she moans at the sweet taste. Her cheeks color, and her whole body warms further. It becomes pliant in my lap, her eyes bright and glowing. I gently pluck the goblet from her hand. She fusses, but I merely shake my head.

"One sip, my blossom, is more than enough for you. Lest the sugarplum wine turn you into one of them." I nod towards the glazed expressions of the humans littered around the clearing. "It will help you relax. Help you let go. Enjoy yourself, I'll keep you safe."

Her smile is brilliant, showing her perfect white teeth. Her expression is all innocence and sweetness. I thought there was no way she could be lovelier, but I was wrong. Laurelle, open and smiling on my lap, is a newfound pleasure. One that rakes its nails down my spine and makes the blood rush in my ears.

I want to devour her whole, but her growling stomach stops me. Plucking a piece of bread off the tray next to me, I bring it to her plump lips. She opens her mouth, her pink tongue inviting as she leans into my side. The softness of her breasts meets the muscles of my chest, and I growl.

Her cheeks color further as she chews and swallows. I feed her more, delighting in the pleasure of caring for her. I bring a few pieces of sugar-coated fruit to her mouth. She moans at the taste, a few sugar crystals collecting at the corner of her mouth. I catch them on my thumb and lick them off.

Laurelle's eyes track the movement. One deep inhale tells me the delicious state her pussy is in. I want to drown in her sweet scent. Fighting the urge to sample the sugar straight from her mouth, I produce a small piece of hard cheese and feed it to her. Over and over again, I give her bits and pieces until she shakes her head.

"I can't possibly eat another bite. I'll burst," she giggles.

Without her walls erected between us, she seems younger—more carefree. I can't help but curl her even deeper against me. She doesn't protest. In fact, one of her arms folds around my shoulders, absentmindedly playing with the strands of my hair.

"Are you feeling better? Was the wine too much?" I ask, needing to know how much that small sip is affecting her.

"I feel...wonderful." Her smile is small and secretive. "This place is—I've never seen anything like it."

"Really? Your human lands don't engage in orgies under the full moon?" I deadpan.

Laurelle chokes on her gasp before giggling. Her side vibrates against mine.

"No, definitely not." She shakes her head, her curls brushing my shoulder. "If my family could see me now, I'm sure they'd drop dead from shock just from how I'm dressed."

Laurelle shakes her head again, breaking out in another fit of giggles. The wine is definitely working. Her tongue is loosening, and I want to use it to my advantage. I'm greedy for any knowledge of her she's willing to share.

"What were they like?" I swallow, unsure if I should ask the next question. "Do you miss them?"

"Miss them?" she laughs. "I—no, I can't say that I do."

"Why?" I ask.

Her eyes grow distant before she speaks again.

"My father was a wealthy man—very wealthy. The fact that he wasn't born into nobility was always a point of contention with him—until recently—I guess that doesn't matter now either." Her fingers curl into one of my locks of hair. "I was merely a pawn to be used for his ambition, a servant to my father's unfettered ego."

"I don't like the idea of you serving anyone but me," I growl, my grip on her tightening.

Sadness dances in her beautiful eyes, shredding my stomach. I hold her tighter and run my hand through her hair. The silky locks slip through my fingers as they reform into perfect spirals.

"They mistreated you," I say softly. Laurelle shrugs, and her eyes move to the debauched scene in front of us once more. Her breath hitches at the sight of those twisting and mashing glowing bodies.

"I had to keep myself hidden and demure in order to fit into their plans. Any inkling of desire was snuffed out and replaced with duty and modesty. My mother said it was the only befitting way for a lady to live. It was the only way I could be worthy of the smarmy prince they wished me to marry."

My claws tighten in her hair. Hot and burning rage laces through me at the thought of another claiming her. Of having her and filling her with this shame she suffers from. Laurelle is a well of desire; I can see it in her eyes, and it begs me to set her free.

I will do it, and I will slay anyone who comes to take her from me.

"You were only meant for a king. Someone with the means to protect you and help guide you in your cravings. That weak mortal prince was never worthy of you. He wouldn't have treated you like the jewel you are—not as I will."

"Hmm," she moans deep in her throat. "Presumptious are you? We barely know each other, yet you've declared I'm yours?"

My claws skim down her back and tangle in her waist.

"Make no mistake, my blossom. You were always mine. I would've found you. Our fates were always meant to intertwine."

Biting her lip, Laurelle's hands explore me. Her speech is clear, and her eyes are bright, telling me the wine has eradicated her apprehension. She's in control of herself and her thoughts. While she may not be drunk by typical human standards, the effects of the wine should not be understated.

However, I see the real her as she sits in my lap—the one I will endeavor to ensure never hides herself in shame. It will be my pleasure to awaken this side of her when the wine is not calling it forth.

My hand skims up her exposed leg, and she shivers. Her fingers trail over my collarbone as I match her breathy moan with one of my own. Her cheeks flush as she explores my jawbone. Warm fingers drag down my throat, then double back to smooth over my cheeks. I want to haul her against me, to meet my mouth with hers and devour her whole. Yet, I hold back and allow her to explore me on her own terms.

When her curious fingers brush against the base of my crown, my groan is ripped from me. Laurelle bites her red lip but doesn't stop. I revel in the comfort she's feeling in touching me. My leaves shift through her hands, the sensation sending a pleasant tingle down my spine. They are a part of me, and as such, they delight in her attention.

"Does it hurt?" my blossom asks, eyes wide as she combs through the foliage on my head once more.

A breath puffs from her full lips in surprise as my crown transforms in her grasp. I don't need to see it to know what it looks like now. Instead of two strong branches, it has become smaller, merely a dusting of fragile twigs and a few leaves woven together. It's lighter in this form, but its significance is still great.

"I was born with it. It will always be a part of me until all of this is nothing but dust and dirt."

She wrinkles her nose slightly before saying, "That sounds like a big responsibility. Did you not have a choice?"

My claws snag around her waist, pulling her in closer and inhaling more of her floral scent. Her bare leg brushes my raging cock, but she says nothing, even as her cheeks fill with more color. My chest feels tight, but when she doesn't move away from my hardness, I let go of a deep sigh.

"*The Great Oak* chose me as its protector. It made me out of its magic. The same magic that made everything around us. It was what I was born to do—what I will always do until the end of time."

Her eyes go round, and her teeth sink into her lower lip. My free hand cups her cheek, and I pull her chin down with my thumb until her mouth opens slightly. How easy it would be to kiss her—how sweet would she taste?

I shake myself.

"What were you born to do, my blossom?"

She tries to shrug, the movement only causing more of her soft hair to brush my chest.

"I don't know," she admits. "To secure a higher social standing for my father? That's all my parents intended for any of their children, but as far as what I wanted for myself...I don't know. I had to let go of my desires—my goals and ambition—a long time ago."

My hand tightens on her cheek at her obvious mistreatment. I will enact revenge on those who put these doubts inside her beautiful head. Those monsters taught her to be timid when she is a wildfire. She is the sun—meant to burn brightly and to be adored by the masses.

And none will be more adoring than me.

"You were born to be here, Laurelle," I say softly, even as doubt begins to creep into her irises. Before she can shift away from me, I continue, "Let me prove it to you. If only for tonight, give yourself over to this place. Dance, eat, run—let yourself revel in what we have to offer."

Her brown eyes blaze with longing before cooling in an instant. My lips twist as her shoulders curl in on herself.

"I'm not sure. I mean—"

My hand frames her jaw.

"You are mine now. Remember that. No one will touch you but me. Ever."

I snarl the last word as she lets out a whimper. A part of me panics, thinking I've scared her, but then I smell it. Her floral scent is deep and inviting—begging me to sink to my knees and throw her legs over my shoulder. To feast between her thighs, right here on my throne, so everyone gathered knows she is mine, and she is their queen.

In time, I shall do just that. For now, I gently help her to her feet and groan at the feeling of her pert nipples brushing against my chest. Standing, she barely reaches the center of my chest. Taking her arms gently, I turn her towards the party around us.

Bodies of all shapes and sizes work together in a symphony of erotic sounds. Sprites and humans twirl and dance while spilling sweet wine into their mouths. The night has only just begun, and it's time for my sweet blossom to enjoy it.

"Go," I say.

She hesitates for a second before nodding. Her feet seem stuck next to me, so I shift my hand lower and swat her gently on the supple mound of her ass. She squeals before her bright eyes find mine. The look of scandal on her face is adorable. Her lips twist into a smile as she shakes her head.

"Enjoy yourself, Laurelle. I'll be watching, so be a good girl, but have fun."

With a deep breath, Laurelle throws one more smile my way before walking into the fray. I watch her dark curls disappear into the crowd. My claws scratch at my chest as she gets further away. This space between us is necessary. I want her to be comfortable here, and she needs to see what all is on offer in my realm.

Secure in the knowledge that she'll be back in my arms before the night is done, I sit back on my throne and watch my little blossom bloom into the wildflower she was born to be.

5

EMRYS

The longer I watch Laurelle dance in my meadow, the more I turn into the primal beast my magic demands I become.

How long have I sat on my throne just taking her in? Hours? Days? I do not know, and I do not care. I could spend the rest of my eternal life enjoying the rush of color flooding her cheeks as she spins on the green grass.

Her hands are high above her head, showing off the perfect, curvy expanse of her body. The sheer gown barely conceals her and a growl worms its way up my throat. Her curly head is thrown back in a rich laugh as she spins faster. Sprites and faeries gather around her, none of them daring to get too close and risking my wrath.

Clever little creatures.

Sweat glistens on her face, and a few pieces of dark hair stick to her temple. She is such a treat. Her body moves like water as she flows with the beat. Laurelle has ingested no more faerie wine, and as I suspected, one mouthful was more than enough for my little blossom.

She's unafraid and unleashed. Sensual in a way I doubt she is even aware of.

My Laurelle was born to be a wanton creature just like me. It's evident in the way she moves. Her laughter tickles my ears as she whirls again before falling to the ground. Her whole chest heaves as she giggles before rising again and continuing her dance.

The sight makes me smile even as my thoughts turn dark.

I'll murder her family for keeping her caged. My claws curl into my palm as I think about how they kept my blossom rigid when she was meant to grow free and wild. There is nothing shameful about desire or about expressing it. There is nothing wrong with enjoying life's pleasures and reveling in them. Needs are meant to be met.

And I will satisfy each one of hers, especially when I take her into the heart of *The Great Oak*.

She is mine. I feel it in my bones—my blood. She is the one I've been waiting for. Together, we will restore this land, but more than that, she will belong to me. As I already belong to her. Waiting is torture, but I must. My queen will only find comfort in my company, and if that means swallowing down this lust until it chokes me, I will do so. I will wait for her to be ready and for her to call to me.

And call to me she will. Over and over again, and I will prove to her why I am the only one who will ever rule her— her heart and soul.

Laurelle's body twists once more in tempo with the music. Her arms come down from above her head, and with them falls one of the straps of her dress. Golden skin sparkles under the moonlight, and my mouth waters to taste her. Her chest heaves as a result of her exertion. The fallen strap leaves the swell of her breast dangerously close to spilling out of the top.

The growl I've been holding in echoes from my lips and reaches her.

She turns fully towards me, her face flushed and her eyes bright. As if she's not seen me in years, her lips pull into a surprised smile as she waves. Gathering her skirts, she rushes along the damp grass back over to me.

Out of breath, she grabs my hand and declares, "You must come dance with me!"

I hesitate for only a moment—not because I do not wish to join her but because I want to revel in her smile, in the warmth and affection on her face as she looks at me. Guarded Laurelle was hard enough to resist, but this Laurelle, who looks at me with curiosity and heat, may break my resolve to be patient.

She gives my hand another squeeze.

"Please," she whines.

Licking over my teeth, I rise from my throne.

"Of course, my blossom."

Laurelle lets out a delighted squeal and yanks me towards the clearing. Damp grass and trampled flowers squish between my toes as we fold ourselves in and amongst the bodies. My subjects dance and couple with a frenzy, but with me now in the mix, their attention turns towards us.

Watching and waiting to see if this is the night I claim her.

The crowd pulses with a new energy. Laurelle looks up at me, her small hand still in mine, and with a small grin, turns her back towards me. I want to demand her eyes remain on mine until the supple curves of her ass press against my hard cock.

I let out a hiss and she giggles.

"This is how I saw the others dancing together. Something tells me a formal two-step dance wouldn't be appreciated here," she says, her voice rising above the music.

Wrapping my arms around her waist, I haul her back against me. She gasps at my hardness but doesn't move away. If anything, she grinds herself closer to me. Her hands circle mine, and I lean down and inhale her floral scent. Our bodies move and mash in time with the upbeat song. The sprite on the fiddle works overtime to get the crowd into a fevered frenzy.

Laurelle arches her back ever so slightly and moves side to side in a deliciously maddening way. Dipping my head lower, I skim my nose up her neck and delight in her small gasp.

"Be careful, my blossom, or I'll take you right here in the middle of my subjects."

I wait for her to shove me away, to say I've gone too far, but she doesn't. Instead, she shivers before twisting around to face me. Her eyes are wide with lust, and her cheeks are rosy and gorgeous. Her hands intertwine behind my neck, and she pushes up on her toes. My hands remain on her waist, stroking her warm skin through the fabric.

"Really?" she asks softly. Her lips are so close for the taking.

"Would you like that? To have the others watch as I lay claim to your little pussy?"

The old Laurelle has been eradicated. That question would've had her fleeing and calling me a disgusting beast. This Laurelle, my queen, only lets out a soft moan. Her hands thread through my hair, and she rubs her hard nipples against my chest.

"I've," she pauses and licks her lips, "always been

curious about these types of things. I never let myself explore with anyone—I never felt safe to. But now...I want to."

"With me?" I must hear her confirm it.

She nods before wrinkling her small nose.

"I sound absurd, don't I? Hours ago, I was about to be given to a cruel prince, and now I'm telling the king of the faeries that he makes me feel safe enough to be pleasured. Is this some trick? A game?"

My hand cups her cheek, and I shake my head.

"No trick, my blossom. You desire me as I desire you. There is nothing to fear or be ashamed of. I will keep you safe, always."

"That's the thing," she says. "I don't even know what to desire. I used to have some idea before, but now I—"

"I'll show you," I growl. "Everything. Things even your human mind couldn't dream up. Pleasure will be pulled from your body. You'll beg me to stop because you don't think you can take anymore, but you will."

She lets out a sweet moan and yanks my head down towards her. Tilting her face up to meet mine, I should kiss her. Should make good on my promise to take her right here and now.

Yet, I won't.

Not after she just revealed to me the depths of her innocence. I won't allow her first time to be witnessed by others. In the future, if it's what she desires, then I'll fulfill her in that way, but not yet.

For now, I opt for the second-best option.

Without warning, I scoop her into my arms and turn us away from the crowd. She makes a noise of protest but clings to me nonetheless as we leave the meadow. With my arms under her knees and along her back, I gaze down into her lovely face. Exhaustion dances in her gold-flecked irises.

"I think you've had enough fun with the faeries for one night," I say, rounding down a corner until my palace comes into view.

"Wait! I want to dance more. And you! I thought we were going to—"

My grip on her tightens as I growl through my teeth. She's too tempting for her own good. Passing through the wooden archway of my palace, I race us down the tile floor until we reach the furthest back bedroom.

This palace felt so empty before. Now, with Laurelle in my arms, it glows with new life.

"Are you going to fuck me tonight?" she asks bluntly.

I can't conceal my surprise at her direct question, and my steps stumble.

"That's not a very ladylike question," I chastise.

Her smile heats my blood as she gives a gentle shrug.

"You're the one who said I was no lady." Biting her lip, she glances down. "And you said you're the only one who gets to touch me."

We make our way into my bedroom. Even though I want to keep her locked to me, I gently set her on her feet at the foot of my bed. It can easily sleep ten full-grown humans. The sheets are made of the softest silks, and the pillows are stuffed with goose feathers. If she hates the gold and green color scheme, I'll get rid of it.

Whatever she wants, I will always make sure she has, except tonight.

"Be sure, my blossom, that I would claim you tonight— all night." She moans at my words, taking a step closer to me. "But that sip of faerie wine has lowered your inhibitions. I want you to have a clear head the first time we lie together."

Laurelle looks scandalized as she shakes her head.

"I'm not drunk!" she declares, crossing her arms over her chest. The picture of a petulant child. An idea sparks in her brown eyes as she drops her hands to the neckline of her dress.

"I'm not drunk," she repeats.

With a forceful tug, she shreds the dress clear down the center. All thoughts empty out of my head as I take in her naked body. The smattering of freckles on her chest and stomach. Her full breasts and her hard nipples are at the center of them. My gaze drops lower to the patch of dark curls hiding the one place I want to be inside of forever.

Her voice is shaky, but her touch is firm as she reaches out and places my claws on her hip.

"I want you, Emrys." My name on her lips, while she's naked, has a trickle of seed seeping from my painfully hard cock. "I've never been so sure of anything in my life."

This is going to be a long, *long* night.

My claws tighten on her hip, my other hand feeling the fleshy swell of her ass and dragging her towards me. Her skin is hot and smooth. I will spend an eternity tasting and memorizing every inch of her.

"In the morning, my blossom," I growl near her mouth, her warm breath bathing my lips. "If you still want me like this when the wine is out of your system, I'll fuck you within an inch of your life."

She thrusts herself more against me as I give her backside another squeeze. Her floral scent grows richer, and I can only imagine the amount of sweetness coating the inside of her thighs.

I drop my hand from her ass and take a step back.

Laurelle's eyes lock with mine as she lets out a particularly adorable growl. Without warning, she shoves hard against my chest and knocks me onto the bed. The cool silk meets my skin as she crawls on top of me.

Her wet cunt cradles me through my thin pants. Rubbing herself back and forth against my hardness, I let out a growl, and my claws find her hips to stop her. More seed leaks from me, and I can't allow that.

I need to save it all for her perfect pussy.

Small hands fall to my chest as her breasts dangle before my eyes. I long to have her hard nipples in my palms—and most definitely in my mouth. Her curls tickle my skin as she leans down into my face. Her lips are pouty as her eyes plead with me.

"Emrys, please, I need you. You were the one who told me to be free," she whines. "You unlocked this part of me I had buried away. I burn for you."

With a growl, I lift her off my lap and toss her to the bed beside me. Not giving her a moment's reprieve, I climb on top of her and skim my nose up her neck. Her hands go to my back and dig into my muscles. My tongue licks up the shell of her ear, and I delight in her sigh.

Pressing my lips against her, I say each word carefully.

"Hold on to that lust, Laurelle. I'll reward you for it." My smile is wicked against the side of her face. "Tomorrow."

Laurelle lets out a scream of frustration and rolls on her side, facing away from me. I laugh but slip off from atop her. Pulling back the sheets, I curl her back to my front and lay my arm along her waist.

Turning her head, she appraises me with unhappy brown eyes.

"You really are a cruel captor," she huffs. "Is this how you decided to punish me for my crimes after all?"

My laugh rubbles from my chest as I pull her tighter against me. Her warmth soaks into my skin and dances with the inferno running through my veins.

"Trust me, my blossom, you're going to thoroughly enjoy being punished by me."

Golden light streams into my face, rousing me from a deep, dreamless sleep.

Never in my life have my muscles been this sore. Last night, I used parts of my body I haven't in a very long time. The dancing, the music, the wine—all of it feels like a dream. As my eyes adjust to the room around me, a small part of my brain still believes this is a dream.

How could it not be?

The utter decadence of last night. The way I had barely been dressed, and yet I moved without a care in the world. My body had twisted and swayed in time with the salacious drums and fiddles. I had sat in the king's lap and touched him with reckless abandon before leading him to the dance floor. It had been me who guided him behind me. Me who had allowed him to touch me in a way I've never allowed another male—human or not—to.

Then he carried me back to this room and—

A strong male arm rests heavily against my bare hip, and I'm shocked back into reality. This is very much real. From my sore muscles to the heat of another body pressing into my spine. My eyes focus on the room around me. It's comprised of gold and green fixtures. A gentle breeze blows through the open window and disrupts the emerald curtains. The bedding is made of fine gold silk, and my head rests on the softest pillow.

There are a few pictures on the walls—sketches of the oak trees and the meadow and even a crude portrait of Emrys himself. I'm sure the sprites had a hand in crafting it. There are a couple of wardrobes and a short table surrounded by velvet-covered chairs.

Emrys breathes deep, his breath tickling my ear, and my face heats as I remember our exchange last night. While the faerie wine heightened my senses, I was not drunk in the typical sense. The night isn't blurry in the slightest. I remember how I had danced with him under the moon-light, how pleasure had slid down my spine at his closeness, especially when his hardness pressed against me.

The same hardness I can feel against my backside now.

I had practically thrown myself at him when we had arrived in this room. Disrobing and grinding against his hard cock, it would've been easy for him to take advantage of my desirous state. Yet he hadn't. How many human men would've been so noble?

A woman's willingness is never of great concern to them.

Yet it had been to Emrys. And if I'm being honest—with fresh morning light pouring into the room—while a part of me is a bit embarrassed at the level of my eagerness, my desires have not changed.

I want him as much as I did last night. He teases these desires out of me. Pleasures and feelings I thought I'd never experience now seem within reach.

It's in the way he touches me—how his black eyes seem so cold but only fill me with simmering heat. The ache he created inside me has only intensified. The wine may have helped loosen me up to the idea of staying here, but now, as I sit sober in the warm morning light, I only wish to continue my exploration of the king.

To see how deep this well of desire goes and allow him to wade through it with me.

I sigh deeply and twist onto my other side to face him. In sleep, his face is relaxed. I take in his magnificent features. Did I think him a monster before? Surely not. He's handsome in a way no human man could ever be. Ethereal and otherworldly, and the sight of him has my inner thighs tingling with awareness.

When he tells me he desires me, I believe him.

The taste of freedom I had last night is heady, and I want so badly for it not to be a trick. For the first time in my life, I want to lower my guard and keep it down. I desire him—want him to pleasure me in the way he threatened to, but do I trust him? It's too soon for me to decide, but I won't hesitate to explore.

Brushing my curls out of my eyes, I tuck the strands behind my ear and slowly extend my finger toward his face. Gently and slowly so as not to rouse him, I explore the strong planes of his face. I smooth over his brow and each angular cheek. He's strong and solid. Being naked in his arms should have me blushing and fighting to cover myself, but I don't want to. I love how his smooth skin feels against mine.

I skim my fingertip down the strong column of his nose. Emrys lets out a breath and tips his head towards my touch. My heart pounds as I trace over the pointed shell of his ear before reaching his crown. While it's made of twigs and leaves, it pulses with life.

The pure power of it hums under my fingers.

How can someone so strong be so gentle with me? In my experience, the more power a man has, the crueler he is. Could this faerie king be different than all the others? Could I be happy here with him? He's already claimed ownership of me. My mind wills me to fight against it—to remind myself that I don't want to be owned by anyone. Yet my heart begs me to give in and enjoy all the entrapments he has planned for me.

Skimming my fingers back over his brow, I'm inclined to listen to my heart. My lips itch to follow the path of my hand. I lick my dry lips and shift closer to him.

Slowly, his dark eyes blink open. We stare at each other for a moment, and I allow his woodsy scent to invade my lungs and cause my body to hum with pleasure. His arm tightens around me before his hand skims up my bare back.

I shiver before whispering, "Good morning."

"Good morning, my blossom. I feared I would wake this morning, and you would only be a delicious dream." Emry's lips twist into a self-satisfied smile. "I'm pleased to have awoken and found that you are very much real and that your sweet pussy is soaking me through my pants."

I gasp as he shifts his hips, and I realize just how entwined we are. My leg is slung over his hip while his thigh presses against my heated center. He rubs me there once and gauges my reaction. I only moan and grind myself down against him.

This unbridled yearning is headier than any faerie wine.

Emrys slides his hand up my back to tangle in my hair. Gripping my head, he tips it back and stares down into my eyes. His desire burns through me, igniting my own further.

"Do you feel the same as you did last night?" he asks softly.

My cheeks heat despite myself, and I dip my chin. He

growls against me, the vibrations rattling my own chest. He forces my head back up to stare at him.

"You will not hide from me anymore, Laurelle." My breath hitches at his command. "Last night, you were a woman who demanded what she wanted. That is who you shall be here. Let me ask you again, and you will answer me with your words. Do you feel the same as you did when I brought you to this room?"

Meeting his gaze, I shake my head. His eyes fill with disappointment, but his grip on me loosens. Before he can misunderstand me, I wrap my arms around his neck and bring my body flush with his.

"The ache is even worse than before, Emrys. I want you —I need you," I whisper against his mouth. "I don't know why, and I don't care. This desire...it feels too right to deny."

His groan tickles my lips as his hands dig into my ass and bring me even closer. Pressed like this, I can feel every rise and fall of his chest. Every cut of his muscles presses into my curves.

Emrys's smile is all sharp teeth as he says, "Your body knows who it belongs to. It's mine to praise, to punish, and to pound. That's what you wanted, after all. That's what you begged me for as you rubbed your little wet cunt on me last night."

My face burns at his crude words but I only nod my head.

"Yes," I sigh, "please take the ache away."

His lips skim over my forehead as we strain against each other.

"As king," he says, "I expect to be awoken each morning with breakfast."

That breaks through my lust, cooling it for a moment. Shame threatens to overwhelm me as I remember once more that I am his prisoner—at the very least, his subject. I guess some things about royalty don't change. We are all meant to serve them in the end.

Shifting slightly back from him, I try to hide my disappointment at his abrupt change in personality.

"What would you like to eat? We had cooks while I lived at home. I can make a few dishes, but nothing—"

I let out a squeak as his claws sink into my hips, and he pulls me up his body. Planting my knees on either side of his head, his soft hair tickles the skin of my inner thighs. In this position, my naked body is exposed to the morning light. The urge to cover myself never comes as my hands come down on the wooden headboard to balance. Looking down, Emrys's black eyes sparkle while the bottom half of his face is dangerously close to my molten center.

My breath catches as he presses his face against me. His nose inhales deeply, and I feel his groan permeate his chest.

"This is the only thing I'll need to eat for the rest of eternity."

I don't get a chance to respond as he gives me one thorough lick. My hands grip the headboard even tighter, and I hear the wood creak beneath my hands. The taste is gentle and exploratory. My thighs clench on either side of his head.

Pleasure sings down my spine at the realization that he wasn't commanding me to be his servant but that he wished to give me pleasure. I've heard about this act from the pages of my novels. I had a lady-in-waiting who whispered about it once and said it was nice but not all that pleasurable.

Her partner must've not known what he was doing because this is the most pleasure I've ever felt. Even the fleeting times I touched myself over the years don't compare. Emrys licks me once more, and I moan, thrusting my breasts forward. His hands skim up my sides and cups one in his hand. He rolls my hardened nipple between his thumb and forefinger.

My curls stick to my back as I through my head back.

His mouth works me over and over again, lick after lick and bite after bite. With broad strokes of his tongue, he focuses in on my clit before licking back down to prod at my entrance gently. It's not long before my hips are working in time with his movements.

"Delicious, my blossom," he growls against my feminine flesh. "Too delicious for mere mortals. Has any man ever had a taste?"

My thoughts are scattered as he continues licking me, but somehow, I manage to find my voice.

"Never. Only you."

"Good girl," he states, his claws sinking into my ass once more. The hint of pain only heights my pleasure. Working my hips, I grind against his face. His nose bumps my clit as he tastes my entrance against and again, swirling his tongue around the whole.

"Look at you, riding my face for all that you're worth. Tell me what you're feeling, Laurelle."

"I—I," I murmur, swallowing against the pleasure racing down my spine and pooling in my stomach. "I feel free."

"What else?" Emrys demands.

I whip my hips against him as he sucks my clit into his mouth. My arousal makes it easier to glide over his face. The wet, sucking sounds of him working me only enhance my pleasure. Despite the soreness in my legs, I could stay in this position forever and let him feast on me.

"Pleasure. I feel so much pleasure I could burst with it," I admit.

"Good girl," he praises again. I preen at his words. "My perfect blossom, do you want to know what you taste like?"

"Yes," I moan, my stomach tightening.

"You taste like sunshine and sugarplums. This pussy is too sweet and perfect. I'll guard it from anyone who seeks a taste of their own. From anyone who seeks to even smell you."

His hands slip from my ass to underneath me. One claw dances around my entrance while his mouth returns to my clit. He swirls it inside of me once, twice, and on the third time, he eases it inside of me.

"Emrys, please, I—"

"Come, my blossom. Flood my face with your sweetness, and watch me swallow it down."

Pleasure races through me, and I erupt. With a scream, my body clenches, and I grind and buck against his face and finger. His finger pumps inside me as I squeeze it. The intrusion is foreign but not unpleasant in the slightest.

I whip my body back and forth and wring every ounce of pleasure from his attention. I feel my come flood from me and cover his face. He doesn't stop working me until my stomach heaves, and I float back into my body.

Emrys growls and nips my clit one last time. With one final pump of his finger, he eases it out of me and cups my hips once more. Breathing deep, my chest rises rapidly as Emrys slides me down his body. Sweat drips down my neck, and a curl is stuck to my temple.

My cheeks warm as I stare at Emrys. His handsome face is shiny with my arousal, and I watch rapt as he licks it off of his lips.

"Best meal I've ever had," he declares with a wink.

Leaning up, I don't know what overcomes me, but I run my tongue through my arousal on his cheek. I taste myself mixed with his salty sweat and moan. My mouth hovers over his and I'm dying for a taste of him.

Emrys groans but merely shakes his head.

"Not yet, my blossom."

"You don't...want to kiss me?" Old insecurities sour my stomach.

"Laurelle, of course I do." His eyes are earnest. "I want to do more than just kiss you, but I can't. Not yet."

"Why?" I ask, my voice sounding wounded.

"I—" My rumbling stomach cuts him off, and his white brows lower. "It doesn't matter now. Let me feed you, my blossom. I must tend to your needs."

I want to protest, but after what we've just done together, I feel relaxed, and I want to be close to him. I want to let him take care of me and keep me safe.

His arms lift me from the bed, and he sets me down gently in front of one of the wardrobes. Opening the heavy doors, he shifts through the barrage of hanging fabrics until he selects a simple blue silk gown. Lifting it over my head, he lets it slide down my body. I watch as his hands go to his pants, and I turn, not sure if I'm ready—or trust myself not to jump on him—to see the cock he's kept concealed from me.

Instead, I wander over to the vanity and find a wide toothcomb, a pot of hair cream, and a ribbon the same color as my dress waiting for me. I smile as I begin detangling my hair. It takes a few tries, but I manage to secure my curls into a loose braid and secure it with the soft ribbon. Flinging it over one shoulder, I look at my reflection.

Something is different about me, but I can't put my finger on it.

Emrys approaches from behind me, his hands resting on my bare shoulders. The dress is only held up by thin straps, and the heart-shaped neckline shows off the tops of my breasts.

"You are the most beautiful thing I've ever seen." His eyes darken. "And now I know from first-hand experience, the sweetest."

My cheeks fill with color even as I rise from the chair and turn to shove him.

"You have a filthy mouth." I try and fail to sound chastising. My voice is far too breathy.

"A filthy mouth?" His mouth presses against my ear, sending a chill down my spine. "You didn't seem to mind when you were grinding your needy clit against it."

I giggle and shake my head.

"You are incorrigible."

"And you are delicious." His lips press against the side of my head. "Come let me feed you."

Taking my hand, he leads me from the room before I pause.

"Wait, do I not need shoes?" I ask, looking down at my bare feet. The grass stains from last night have mysteriously disappeared. I glance towards Emrys's naked feet before meeting his amused eyes.

"There's no need for shoes in my realm."

That's the most wonderful thing I've heard in my entire life.

7

LAURELLE

With my hand locked in the faerie king's, he guides me from his room and into the hall.

Our bare feet smack lightly against the tile. The whole palace is filled with golden light filtering in from the carved windows. The fact that we are inside a tree really demonstrates the grandeur of Emrys's magic and how free-flowing it is in this realm. I try to take in as much as possible, but many ornate doors are shut.

A few sprites fly in from the window as we continue down the hall. Their thin wings buzz as they soar towards us. Glowing bodies barely bigger than my finger dance in front of my face before weaving themselves into my curls. A few perch on my shoulders and whisper riddles into my ears.

"The time has come," one whispers. "It must be done."

"Lest our realm turns to muck," another adds, "you and the king must fu—"

"Be gone," Emrys commands, waving a clawed hand through my curls and disrupting the sprites. His dark eyes blaze with authority. Even the few sprites collecting on his shoulders follow his command—their colorful bodies cooling to paler shades.

"The sister said something similar. What am I meant to do for you?"

Unease tickles my stomach. Am I no more than a pawn to Emrys as well? Is he using me for his own means, just as my father did?

Emrys is quiet as he leads me through a set of wooden doors. They are ornately carved with pictures of oak trees and a pair of antlers circling above them in a simple replication of Emrys's crown. Gently, the king takes my arm and helps me to the table. It's a long, glistening creation comprised of pale-colored wood. Around it sit ten velvet chairs, but only two place settings are arranged across from each other at the middle of the table.

The king pulls out my chair, and I slip onto it. I wait for him to move to his own seat until I feel his claws on my shoulders. Giving them a gentle squeeze, I look up at him. His face is earnest, his dark eyes swimming with a depth of emotion.

"All I want from you right now, Laurelle, is to feed you and make you happy. What my subjects keep pestering you about isn't something I want you worrying about."

"But I will worry if you aren't honest with me." My voice is small but clear.

"Soon, my blossom. All will be revealed, but for now, I need you to eat."

With a wave of his hand, platefuls of delicious-smelling food cover the table. There are several jars of fresh jam in all different colors. Dark and light-colored bread lay steaming inside towel-covered baskets. There's an array of fried meats and soft cheeses.

My apprehension is quickly forgotten as my stomach growls loudly.

Emrys rounds the table and stands across from me. Reaching out, his claws clink on the ceramic plate as he begins piling food high on my plate. My tongue licks over my lips as I watch him expertly butter a piece of brown bread before laying a glossy helping of scrambled eyes on top. This is a feast even my wealthy father would be envious of.

The glass goblet in front of me fills with a pale gold liquid. I raise my brow at Emrys as he sets my overflowing plate in front of me.

"Apple juice," he explains.

I giggle despite myself. It's such a mundane drink for somewhere so...otherworldly. Or is it laced with something like the wine had been? I grip my fork and meet his stare again.

"Is it...like the wine? And the food, will it make me drunk like last night?"

"No," he says, piling a helping of bacon onto his own plate.

"Do a lot of humans live here?"

I remember the ones I had seen last night. Their eyes milky and unseeing. Their mouths open in erotic sighs—drunk on wine and pleasure.

"Only naughty ones." Emrys's grin is wicked, and it sends a thrill down my spine.

One glance at his mouth, and I remember how it felt against me. How his tongue had tasted and feasted on my most private flesh. How I had ridden—

I cough before taking a small sip of my juice. The crisp tartness explodes on my tongue. There's no need to get carried away with those thoughts already. Besides, I am starving.

I devour my pile of eggs and take a few bites of the cured ham. The salty taste leaves me in need of something sweet. Reaching for a pot of red jam, I slather it on a buttered roll and take a bite. The jam is thick and sugary as it coats my tongue. It takes of strawberries and some other fruit I can't place.

Moaning again, I say to Emrys, "This is delicious."

He chuckles darkly. "I'm sure it's only second in sweetness to your pussy."

My face warms, and I shake my head. "You don't talk like a king."

His grin is all teeth. "Then all the kings you've met must have been quite boring."

I nod. They were nothing like Emrys. Not as caring or considerate. They didn't look at me as if I hung the moon in the sky or was the sun in which his world orbited. No, they looked at me—at everyone—only to assess how they may be of value.

My father may not have been a king, but he was cut from a similar cloth.

Unease rakes its icy nails down my spine as I think back to how Emrys avoided my question earlier. As much as I want to trust him, a small bit of apprehension holds me back. My heart screams at me to submit to him fully, but my mind can't stop questioning everything.

Setting my fork down, I take another sip from my crystal goblet before squaring my shoulders.

"Emrys, what is meant to happen to me here?" I ask.

"You belong to me." His answer is quick. "Your place is here with me, forever, as is your punishment for plucking my flower."

Again, I raise a brow and gesture towards the table.

"This doesn't seem like much of a punishment."

Emrys's grin deepens. "Punishments can always be pleasurable."

I smile slightly before biting my lip and looking away.

"Why not turn me into one of the other humans? What's all this talk from the sprites? The sisters said I was different. What are they talking about?"

The king shakes his head, his white hair floating around his shoulders.

"I don't want you thinking about that. It's not—"

"Please," I interrupt. "Please, be honest with me, Emrys. I want to trust you, but I can't if you are keeping secrets from me."

I know it's quite a demand to make of a king who has ruled for centuries. To demand he lay all of his truths at my feet is laughable. However, I have to know. I can't enter into any sort of relationship with him without understanding my true purpose for being here.

After a moment, Emrys sighs and rubs a clawed hand down his face.

"This is going to be a problem," he sighs.

My heart pounds. "What is?"

"You, my blossom," he says, "when you use that word. When you beg me so prettily, I find I can deny you nothing."

"Oh," I say. "Well, good?"

"Good," he chuckles. "You're going to bring me to my knees, Laurelle. Never has anyone had this much power over me."

My lips twitch even as my cheeks warm. "I'm sorry?"

Emrys laughs and reaches towards me. His thumb wipes at the corner of my mouth and comes away sticky with remnants of my strawberry jam. Licking it off his finger, he groans.

"Too sweet for your own good," he states. "Alright, my blossom, I will tell you all you need to know. In due time."

"But—"

"I know that's not what you want to hear, but I promise you will not make any decision without being fully informed. Do you trust me? At least in that regard?"

My throat feels dry. To take this leap of faith with a faerie king, no less, is asking a lot. Yet Emrys has shown me more kindness and understanding than anyone in a long time. I owe it to him to extend the same courtesy, at least for the time being.

"I do," I respond. "But I want to know the full truth before long."

Emrys nods. Looking around the room, his dark eyes connect with mine. They've cooled a bit, and I watch him inhale a great breath.

"Do you want to return to the world above?"

The question is asked so softly that I almost don't hear it. At the abrupt turn in the conversation, my heart kicks up as I consider his question.

"If I said yes, would you let me go?"

Emrys's eyes flash and his pale lips flatten into a hard line.

"I wouldn't," he pauses, "I wouldn't like it. A part of me says no. It says that I would chain you to my bed before I ever let you leave."

I suck in a breath, but the king continues.

"Yet, I know I couldn't do that. To cage you—even to keep you—isn't something I could stomach." His eyes pour into my mind as if he can see my very soul. "Know this, Laurelle, if the time comes when you want to return above, I will let you go. It will always be your choice to stay with me or not."

"To stay with you and be punished with orgasms and bountiful breakfasts?" I ask.

Emrys barks a laugh, the tension leaving his shoulders. "Exactly."

I think about his question. When I first arrived, I would've seized this opportunity to leave. Was my arrival only a night ago? Regardless, I was content on biding my time and escaping as soon as the moment presented itself.

Yet, now that it's been dangled in front of me, I no longer want it. It's not because I feel under the influence of any magic or wine. No, it feels as if I know Emrys. Like we've spent weeks together rather than just a night.

It's strange, but I don't want to leave for now. Besides, I have nowhere to go back to.

"My family will wonder what happened to me." My body shudders. "I don't even want to think of how the prince will react when I don't show up for our engagement."

The king raises and brow and asks nonchalantly, "Would his head ease your concerns?"

My mouth drops open. Surely, he is kidding. He has to be. To imply that he would—

"I'll kill him for you, my blossom. You need only say the word," he continues.

Shock ices over my veins. I knew Emrys was powerful, but to show it in this way...I should be appalled at the depths of cruelty and be standing to flee—demand he take me to the above world. I shouldn't feel warmth spread throughout my stomach and pool between my thighs.

"You would do that?" I ask, my voice barely above a whisper.

"There's nothing I wouldn't do to give you peace of mind."

I consider his offer before shaking my head. "That's not necessary. Whatever anger the royal family feels towards my disappearance can couple with my family's. For the first time, I didn't do exactly what they wanted. I wasn't the perfect, dutiful daughter forsaking her own desires in order to help my father reach his."

Emrys's dark eyes bore into mine.

"What did you desire, Laurelle? Back when you were able to dream?"

I bite my lower lip and think back. When I was a young girl, I had been afforded a bit more freedom. Before I became of age, I still had to hold myself to a high standard, but I was still young enough not to face the entire scrutiny of my mother and father. I remember summers spent in the garden, reading all manner of tales under the warm sun. I remember wanting so badly to have adventures like theirs.

To find true love that only seemed to exist inside those pages.

That is my deepest desire. The only desire I've held on to even when all hope seemed lost. Can I really share that with the king? Will he think me foolish? Does true love even exist for faeries? Lust and ownership are clearly present, but what about something beyond that?

I huff a laugh and shake my head, falling back on my old training to keep some secrets to myself.

"It's ridiculous—frivolous nonsense. A childish desire."

Emrys's eyes harden, and his mouth thins.

"If it's something you want, then it isn't nonsense."

"It's nothing, really," I say, trying to end this line of questioning.

"Tell me," he commands.

"No," I snap. His eyes flash and I have to look away. I'm not angry with him. Truth be told, I'm not even upset. The reminder of what I've always wanted—even in a place like this—seems still out of my reach. If my lust for Emrys turned into love, would his infatuation do the same? Or will I always be his pleasured prisoner? Something to be kept and not to be treated as the other part of his soul like I desire.

Why am I already considering loving a faerie king I barely know?

"Laurelle." His voice is soft like spring rain. "Please tell me. Whatever it is, I will not find it foolish, I swear to you."

Licking over my dry lips, I hesitate once more. Can I really do this? Trust him with this deep desire? My parents both drilled into me that it was a foolish want. That I should be ashamed for even wishing for such things when my purpose was to make connections—to gain power for my family. Is that why I am so afraid to tell him? To have my parent's sentiments be echoed by his own?

Giving myself no chance to reconsider, I jump off the cliff and wait for the sea of my truth to swallow me whole.

"Love," I whisper. "True love, the kind from legends and tales. That's all I've ever wanted in life."

I hold my breath and do my best not to avert his intense gaze. Something shifts in his dark eyes. They fill with a new light. His mouth parts, revealing some of his sharp teeth. He's handsome—so handsome that it makes me ache anew. There's danger written in every line of his face, yet his eyes show his true, gentle nature.

Seconds pass and then minutes. I wait for him to laugh at me—mock me as my parents have. I don't expect him to slide his black-tipped hand across the table and cover mine. The silky warmth of his skin causes more fire to roar in my blood. Gently, he squeezes my hand as a small smile plays on his lips.

"Then I will earn you love, my blossom," he declares. "It will be the sweetest thing I've ever claimed."

Shock has me stumbling over my words.

"I—Emrys, that's not entirely what I—"

"If I prove myself worthy of your love, will you stay with me? Claim this as your home for all eternity? Will you give me the chance to earn your trust and safeguard your heart?"

My mind races. I had expected Emrys to say...anything else. For him to plead with me to earn my love...isn't this exactly what I've always wanted? Sure, he may not be a shining knight coming to rescue me from a locked tower, but he is in a sense my savior.

By plucking his flower, I was saved from my cruel husband-to-be.

In return, I now have my own king, giving me pleasure and treating me with kindness. Do I not owe it to myself and to him to see if this can blossom into more?

Before I can answer, Emrys pushes back from the table. Rounding it in the blink of an eye, he falls to his knees beside me. Turning my chair, he clasps my hands in my lap. In this position, our faces are nearly the same height.

"I'll give you everything, my blossom. Every want and whim of your heart, I will lay them all at your feet. Pleasures unknown to mortal kind, I will bestow on your beautiful body. All the freedom you can dream of will be granted to you, so long as you share my bed every night."

I shiver at his words. My thighs clench together.

"Why would you do all that? If I am meant to serve you already as my punishment, surely there is no need to...earn my affection." Why am I trying to fight this? Have I been so conditioned that my body's response is to fight even when presented with what it desires most?

Glancing away, my face warms as I say, "After last night and this morning, you see how willing I am to share your bed already."

Emrys growls, his hands tightening over mine.

"Lust and pleasure are one thing, Laurelle. Both of them are important things, but they are fleeting. Love—like the kind you dream of having—is for eternity. I have searched for it myself over the years and never thought I would find it. And then you fell into my realm, and I realized that I had been waiting for you all this time."

Tears prick my eyes.

"Emrys—"

"I've had centuries to prepare for you. Experiences that make me certain of who and what you are to me. You have not had that luxury. Let me earn it—let me show you that I am worthy. Let me show you what could be yours if you choose to stay with me." One clawed hand cups my cheek and forces my eyes on him. "As for your...service to me—the whispering from my meddling subjects—I will explain all of that to you in time."

I nod my head, accepting his words, as I stare at the truth in his dark eyes.

"A noble king puts his realm's needs before his own, but I will not put their needs above yours." His words send a hot trick down my spine. "When I claim you in the way I have wished since the moment you dropped from the sky, it will be because you beg me to. You will commit yourself to me— bind yourself to me—and fulfill the prophecy of your own free will. And you will do it because I have earned it."

"Prophecy?" I ask. The sister never mentioned anything like that.

"All will be revealed later, my blossom. For now, let me commence with making all your wishes come true."

I can't help but chuckle. Rising from the floor, he gently pulls me with him. I crane my neck back to stare up at his face. Twisting one of my brown curls around his finger, he raises a white brow.

"Tell me something you wish to do. Anything, and I will make it yours."

I consider his words. Going back into my mind, I try to remember the young girl I once was. If she was given unbridled freedom, what would she have wished for? The realization shocks me like a bucket of cold water. I can smell her choice. Salt on the air and hot sand pooling between my bare toes.

Only this time, my mother won't be here to condemn me for getting the bottom of my gown wet.

Biting my lip, I smile up at my faerie king.

"I really want to go swimming."

8

EMRYS

Laurelle was made for the sun.

Her soft skin welcomes the heat of its rays. Standing along the sandy shore, crystal blue water laps at our feet. It's shockingly cool against the humid temperature.

A gentle, salty breeze blows a few of her curls that cling to her temples. A cluster of white birds caw overhead, and I can see a pair of sparkling fish swimming close to shore a couple of feet away. I rarely come here. This part of my realm is tucked away—far from the prying eyes of my subjects. What *The Great Oak* needed with a beach, I do not know, but I've never been more grateful for it.

Whisking Laurelle here and watching her brown eyes glow with excitement had been worth it. Her plump lips remain slightly parted as she takes in the rising tide. My blood screams to kiss her—to lay her out on the sand and claim her in a soul-connecting way that would leave no questions about my devotion to her.

My new goal quells my rampant lust. Earning her love.

The meadow has been dying for years at this point.

What will waiting a little longer to complete the ritual with Laurelle hurt? Especially when the prize at the end is as sweet as my blossom.

Does she think her desire for love is foolish? It is not. If only she knew that I am way passed loving her. I'm obsessed —hungry and all-consumed by her mere presence.

Not just for her body, even though I can't wait to be inside of her and feel her smooth thighs against my hips. I'm obsessed with her. I want to hold her down and demand she tell me everything she's ever felt. Every thought she's ever had. I want to know her fears, her dreams, and above all else, her desires.

My chest feels tight at the thought of her. Her beauty is beyond compare. Especially now, as she sparkles in the sun. Her body is soft and supple, her curves highlighted in her thin dress. The hem of which is already covered in sand.

"This is so lovely," she sighs, her sweet voice catching me off guard. I want to swallow the sound of it. "How is it possible? For us to be this far underground, how is there a full ocean?"

My mouth twists into a grin as I look down at her.

"Anything is possible in the faerie realm. Magic makes it so."

Laurelle giggles, and her hands go to the tie on her braid. Gently, she pulls the silk ribbon free and shakes out her curls. Raking her fingers through her hair, she gathers it at the top of her head before twisting it into a loose knot. Her hands work to secure the ribbon around the bun once, then twice, to no avail.

I chuckle before capturing her hands with my own. Using my claws to scratch her scalp she sighs. Twisting my wrist, I reform the bun before tying it securely with the ribbon. A few loose curls cling to her graceful neck and along the sides of her face.

I can't help myself, and I lean down to inhale more of her floral scent. I meant what I said before: she's too sweet for her own good.

Blushing, Laurelle smiles up at me.

"Thank you," she says.

I nod and gesture towards the water. "Ready to go in?"

Laurelle wrinkles her nose and says, "Actually, I thought we could just sit here for a bit."

I watch as Laurelle sits down on the white sand. Her toes dig into the ground as she sighs. I follow suit, sinking down next to her and allowing our bare shoulders to brush. The water comes racing towards us and spills over the tops of our feet.

We breathe in comfortable silence. Have I ever felt this content in the centuries I've been alive?

Laurelle's eyes close as she lifts her face to the sun. A single bead of sweat glides down her forehead, and my tongue is eager to taste it. I have to dig my hands into the sand to keep from grabbing her. My blossom tortures me in the best way.

"My mother never let me sit in the sun this long," Laurelle says, breaking me from my salacious thoughts. "Thought it would age me prematurely."

I chuckle. "Never fear. The faerie world will keep you just as you are now."

Lifting my hand from the grand, I gently trace a claw down her graceful neck. Snagging on her collarbone, I savor her sharp inhale.

"Besides, wrinkles or not, you'd still be the most beautiful woman in existence."

My claw slides over her soft shoulder and underneath

the delicate strap of her dress. With a gentle push, it slips off her shoulder. I quickly give the other one the same treatment. The two green straps rest against her upper arms, and while I'd love nothing more than to continue until her breasts are bare, I don't.

"Tan lines," I explain at Laurelle's raised brow.

She smirks and shakes her head.

We remain quiet on the sand for a long time. The rushing of water and the gentle calling of birds lull us both into relaxation. The sun overhead soaks into my bones, making my muscles loose. I inhale the saltwater and Laurelle's scent and feel nothing but peace. The worries and stress of my kingdom are gone—there is only her.

I watch Laurelle through heavy lids. Her face is flushed, and sweat beads along her temple. It glides down her neck and soaks the top of her gown. She fans the back of her neck, even as she continues to bask in the sun's warmth.

"You can take your dress off," I offer.

Even with her eyes closed, she smiles at my words. "You'd like that, wouldn't you."

"No need to play demure, my blossom." I lean closer to her side and whisper the words near her ear. "I've already tasted your sweet pussy, and you all but begged me to fuck in you in front of everyone gathered in the meadow."

Her golden-flecked eyes slide to mine.

"You were very kingly in the way you put a stop to my wanton advancements."

My smile is all teeth.

"My resolve is stronger than most. Even if your temptation was more than I could bear."

Her face turns from me but I softly grip her chin and force her eyes back on me.

"You don't have to hide. Any part of you from me. My

desire for you is evident and unending. You can revel in it without worrying that it will dissuade me or that it may tempt me to go farther than you'll allow." I squeeze her chin. "You are the only thing that matters to me, Laurelle. You decide the pace between us. Whatever you wish to give me, I am more than eager to have."

She considers my word, her head tilting to the side. I watch her chest rise and fall rapidly before lifting her small hands to the top of her dress. With one smooth motion, the silk slips down her body, baring her breasts. She tugs it the rest of the way and pulls it off at her feet.

I suck in a breath. I've seen her naked—and tasted her sweet flesh just this morning. However, it's like seeing her for the first time. Her skin glows as she meets my gaze. I nearly come in my pants at the defiant look she's giving me. Free and confident.

Her breasts are perfect, round, and more than a handful. Her hips flare before tapering into her shapely thighs. Her nipples harden under my gaze. My eyes only dip lower to her pretty little cunt hiding between her legs.

Taking the dress from her, I lay it on the ground beside us. I shed my own pants, wanting to be as naked as her. Waving my hand, I motion for her to lie atop her dress while I fall to the warm sand beside her.

Stretching beneath the sun, my mouth waters as I take in every line of her body. I count the freckles on her cheeks and chest. A small smile curves her mouth as she rolls onto her front.

"This feels very wicked," she sighs, her ass thrust into the air.

My cock hardens, rising up to brush against my stomach. Her eyes drift there, her flushing face the only indication that she's pleased by what she sees. That and her deepening scent. If I reached between her legs, I knew she'd be soaked for me.

Skimming my claws down her soft skin, I trace the indentation of her spine. Goosebumps break out along her flesh as she sighs.

"Is this okay?" I whisper. At her nod, I continue.

I trail my hand lower, over one cheek of her ass. I give it a gentle squeeze as her thighs clench together. Not trusting myself to get any closer to her wet flesh, I double back and run my claws up her side.

Laurelle lets out a breathy giggle and squirms away from my touch. A soft laugh escapes my lips, and I brush up her side once more. She groans and flails her legs.

"Are you ticklish, my blossom?" I chuckle.

"Yes!" she cries, trying in vain to escape my fingers. "Will you torment me with this knowledge?"

My grin deepens as I lift off the ground.

"Perhaps," I say and double my efforts.

Using both my hands to touch her. I skim up her sides and her hips and even reach beneath her to the soft curve of her stomach. She thrashes in my grip, rolling onto her back to shove me off as she laughs. Tears form in her eyes as she babbles and tries to push my tormenting hands away. Her legs tangle with mine.

With her thighs open, I settle between them as my hands fall to either side of her head. Our chests meet as we breathe in deep. Both of us are acutely aware of how close we are. How easy it would be for my cock to slip inside her. How her hot cunt is warming it even now as if inviting me to take her.

Our lips are barely a breath apart. Her hands come up to my sides and curl into my shoulder blades. Her brown eyes are alluring—encouraging me with no words to kiss her. I wait for her to command me, yet it doesn't come.

That's the only reminder I need before I get too carried away.

Pressing a kiss to her forehead, I pull back.

"I'm being a poor host."

Laurelle lowers her dark brows as I nod towards the water.

"You said you wanted to swim, and we haven't even taken a step into the water."

Sinking her teeth into her lower lip, Laurelle averts my eyes.

"Oh, I don't mind. Laying in the sun suits me better anyway."

When her eyes meet mine again, I see the wariness clouding them. Her mouth mumbles something about there being sharks or other creatures who could eat her. I shake my head, gently pulling back from her body.

"The Kraken knows better than to send his vermin to my realm. The water is safe. I promise."

Still, the wariness remains in her eyes.

After a moment, it clicks. My hand is gentle on her arm as I pull her up and brush the sand from her soft skin. I keep my voice even and meet her gaze.

"Can you swim?"

Laurelle grimaces and looks away. Capturing her face in my hand, I don't let her hide from me. After a moment, she sighs and shakes her head.

"One of our servants taught me when I was little. We'd sneak off to do it at this small pond right outside my family's manor." She wrinkles her adorable nose. "That was until my mother found us and forbade me from ever doing it again.

The next morning, that servant girl was sent to who knows where."

After another beat of silence, Laurelle continues.

"I thought being here—doing this—would be the first step in reclaiming some of the freedom that was stolen from me. But now...looking at the water...it's so much bigger than the pond where I learned. What if I've forgotten or—"

Rising to my feet, I offer her my hand.

"I'll teach you. You're safe with me."

Laurelle hesitates before I feel her skin slide against mine. Pulling her to her feet, I walk her towards the open water. We both let out a yelp as the cool water reaches our knees, then our hips. Being a good foot taller than her, I can still stand long after she can't. Once the water hits her shoulders, I grip her waist in my hands.

"Kick your feet and your arms at the same time, that will help you stay afloat."

She does so. Her legs brush mine as she treads water. The foamy spray tickles my nose as I hold fast. My feet drag along the sandy bottom as she continues to move in my grip.

"Move with the water, not against it."

Slowly, her moves are less silted and more fluid. She glides against the incoming waves. I watch her long limbs slash through the calm surface as she keeps herself upright. She barely notices when my hands leave her skin. Laurelle's face is a picture of concentration as she keeps herself above water.

Her face turns back towards me and she gasps, her efforts failing when she sees how far I've let her drift from me. I'm at her side in an instant, helping her regain her leverage and floating once more.

"You're doing so good, Laurelle." Her cheeks warm at my praise.

She kicks her legs before lying on her back. The water keeps her body buoyant as I float beside her. The sun has brought more freckles to her nose, and I count them. Saltwater collects on her dark lashes.

"I used to do this before my mother caught us. I'd float in the sun wearing only my shift," she admits. "I'd dream of a life where I could do this forever—where there were no rules."

Her eyes blink open towards me. "I never could've dreamed you or this place up. Not in a million years."

My hands find her waist once more and pull her into my arms. Her legs wrap around my hips as we stare at each other. Tendrils of her hair cling to her face, and I brush them back with a claw. Her breasts press against my chest, and suddenly I'm overwhelmed with greediness again.

I want to fulfill her in every way I can. I have to.

"What else did you dream of doing?"

She shifts against me, her pussy brushing my hard cock and eliciting a groan from me. Her dark eyes sparkle as we stare at each other. Wrapping her arms tighter around my neck, her head fits perfectly in the groove of my shoulder. Her mouth moves dangerously close to my own.

"I dreamt hundred of dreams in that pond," she confesses. "I dreamt of baking enough pies to fill a whole room. Of having a library with a million books. Of being able to paint with an unlimited supply of colors. To count the stars until the sun came up."

She pulls back, a small smile on her lips.

"Silly nonsense, you see."

My grip on her tightens. I squeeze her sides until her eyes meet mine again.

"Easily met demands for a faerie king," I correct.

Her smile is beautiful enough that my chest begins to

hurt. Once more, I am renewed with purpose. My queen has given me a list of demands, and I will see each one fulfilled.

Her pussy grazes me once more. The pleasure of being inside of her will destroy and remake me. I will be a new king after filling her with my seed and claiming her as my own. For now, in this moment, it is more than enough for her to look at me like she is. With openness in her eyes and a soft smile on her lips.

To share in her joy and know that I am the lucky male who procured it for her.

I'll win her smile every day. I'll be worthy of it. Giving her waist another squeeze, I slide my hands along her sides until she's breathless and thrashing once more.

"We'd better get started," I whisper in her ear. "We have a long day of making all of your dreams come true."

"There," I say, wiping my flour-covered hands on my smock.

The white powder mixes in with the paint stains already smeared across the front. After we finished our swim in the sea, Emrys took me back to his tree palace and let me wash the salt and sand from my skin and hair. Despite asking him to join me in the tub, Emrys merely growled before kissing me on the forehead and saying he had things to attend to.

I scrubbed away my disappointment—and lust-filled frustration—with a bar of jasmine soap. Once I was dry, I slipped on a new, fresh dress. This one was light pink and silky with thin, short sleeves. It clung to my chest before flaring out to a fuller skirt around my waist.

When the king reappeared, I had just finished twisting my curls away from my face.

Without so much as a word, he merely took my hand in his and led me down the golden hallway. We walked in comfortable silence until we paused outside of a set of double doors. With a wave of his claws, they both swung open and revealed the most incredible sight I had ever seen.

A small room illuminated by a stained glass window opened to let in the fresh smell of the meadow below. There was an easel and an endless supply of blank canvases. They ranged in size and lined the stone walls. Stacks of sketchbooks with pencils and pens were collected in cups beside them.

However, the shelves along the far wall were the most marvelous. They were easily seven feet tall, and I noted a small wooden stool had been provided for me to reach the top. Easily two feet deep, they were filled to the brim with every color imaginable.

Dark purples bled into vibrant teals that turned into hazy blues. Golden yellow, sunshine yellow, and daisy yellow covered another shelf. There were so many colors—some of which I'd never seen before—that my eyes could barely take them all in.

I turned towards Emrys, his dark eyes glowing.

"Is this what you dreamed it would be like? To paint with never-ending colors?" he asked softly, waving a claw toward the room. He seemed to hold himself still in anticipation of my answer.

There were no words to describe this wonder. No words seemed appropriate to thank him, so I merely pressed my lips to his cheek and gave his hand a squeeze.

It was all a blur as I sat down in front of the easel. Emrys asked me what I wanted to paint first, and after a moment, I thought of my answer.

In my mind, I saw a river—great and roaring—while above it, the sun began to set, casting the world in dark purples and warm pinks. I told Emrys of my vision and gasped when he wiggled his fingers. Just beyond my easel, I watched the stone wall adorned with the stained glass transform into my sunset scene. It was real enough that I swore I could feel the mist from the water.

I didn't dare ask how it was possible because I already knew. Magic. Such wonderful, splendid magic.

Emrys used his powers to help me paint vision after vision. From my family's estate—cast in dark colors and rainclouds—to Emrys's palace—warm and golden. I don't know how much time had passed before I stopped. My fingers ached from holding the brush, and my back was feeling tight.

My faerie king had watched me contently from his place on the stool beside me. He didn't offer critiques of my novice art skills. In fact, he praised my color choices, causing my face to tingle throughout the afternoon. A few sprites had breezed in, tangling in my hair and smearing the paints on my palette before Emrys ran them off when they started whispering riddles about the prophecy.

I welcomed their company, but my king seemed to be in no mood to share my attention.

That had sent a pleasant thrill through me. I loved his unbridled attention—the heat in his gaze. I even enjoyed the chaos and frenzy of his world. It was intoxicating being surrounded by so much life and magic. Emrys himself was intoxicating.

After my paintings were left to dry on the wooden tables, Emrys fed me meat and cheese until my strength was renewed. My eyelids felt heavy for a moment before he helped me from the painting studio, down the hallway, and through another set of doors.

Behind which sat the kitchen of my dreams.

Spacious and open, the stove and oven are made of white stone, and the counters are carved from golden quartz. The fires were already roaring by the time we entered, and my eyes snagged on the workbench in the center of the room. It was stacked full of ingredients for every type of pie.

Candied fruits and melted chocolate were set next to roasted chicken and vegetables, depending on whether I wanted to make a sweet or savory pie. There were fresh crust rolled out and hundreds of pie dishes to bake my creations in.

That is where I have spent this whole evening.

With Emrys by my side, we roll out the dough before more is magically made for the next pie. We place it gently in the dish before filling it with whatever concoction I'm feeling. Emrys uses his claws to pinch the sides, while I use excess dough to create a design on top.

I've just fasted the wildflower-shaped dough over the top of my glossy blackberry pie when a buzzing sound goes off. With a wave of his claw, the oven doors open for Emrys, and the latest batch of pies fly out on a sweet-smelling cloud. They land with a soft thud on the counter to cool while our new batch replaces them.

They smell delicious, but the king and I have eaten so many slices over the past few hours that I can't possibly ingest anymore. I told Emrys it felt wasteful, but he assured me these pies would be offered to his hungry subjects in the meadow.

I glance down at the pies fresh from the oven. The chicken pie bubbles up through the lattice top. Its rich gravy containing carrots and celery makes my mouth water despite my fullness.

Emrys's soft steps echo behind me while his claws dig softly into my waist. I sigh and snuggle back into his body. Have I ever felt this content? This safe? Everything I've ever dreamed of, he's brought to me. All day, he's catered to my every whim, listened to my every word, and given me something I haven't had in a long time.

Happiness.

More odd still is I feel like I know the faerie king. Something in my heart tells me that I do. Throughout our time together, we've talked and shared stories. I revealed more of my time living under my father's thumb, and Emrys made several offers to bring me his head as well. Again, I told him it wasn't necessary.

Just being able to confess to my mistreatment had me feeling lighter.

A closeness has formed between us. One that makes me feel as though we've spent lifetimes together, and I should embrace these feelings. My soul belongs to him—or at least it wants to.

How can I feel this way after only a day?

Albeit one full day. My body is bone tired. It's lived a dozen lives between swimming this morning to putting these final pies in the oven. A yawn sneaks up on me as I watch the sun through the glass window finally begin to dip and darken.

Gently, Emrys's claws go to the tie at my back. Once the smock is loose, he slips it over my head and turns me in his arms. Using his thumb, he gently wipes some flour from my cheek. I smile up at him, the small gesture feeling extremely intimate.

"Did you enjoy today?" His voice is rough with desire.

"Yes," I say, wrapping my hands around his neck and molding my body to his. "Doesn't it feel like we've spent weeks together?"

Emrys chuckles, and his hands skim up my sides. My thighs clench together as more heat licks up my spine. The longer I stare into his eyes, the more truth spills passed my lips and pools on the floor between us.

"I want you," I sigh. "I want to give myself to you."

I want to love you. The thought steals my breath as I manage to conceal that final confession.

Emrys lowers his face to the top of my head and inhales deeply.

"I'd be a poor king if I did not inform you that time moves differently here, my blossom."

Leaning back, I look up into his handsome face with a raised brow.

"Moves differently, how?"

His claws skim down the side of my face.

"Faster or slower, depending on my mood."

My heart pounds, and I lick my dry lips.

"How...how long have I been here?"

His smile is small, but I notice the way his body stiffens.

"By human standards, maybe..." he hesitates. "Three weeks? A month at most."

The world around me freezes. The warmth of the ovens only adds to the heat of my body. His words bounce around in my head. Three weeks? No more than a month? He can't be serious. He can't mean—

"I've known you a month?" I choke out.

"Only in human time," he reminds me.

I wait for the shock to render me motionless. I wait for anger to course through me and propel my arms to shove away from him. Yet, nothing like that happens because...I don't care. This has been the most wonderful day—month, I guess—I've ever had. Beyond how kind he's been to me, I feel the rightness of us in my bones.

Knowing him for a month doesn't feel like a shock. It feels...*right*.

This also clears up one of my last hesitations. We've known each other a month in my world, that's more than enough time to give my body the last push it needs into this waiting pool of desire. I've known my faerie king longer than it takes some people to be married. There's no need to hold back when it comes to each other.

Not that I've been doing that since last night.

My hands tangle into his hair. I scratch at his scalp until his rigid posture melts into my curves. His hands on me tighten, causing more moisture to pool between my thighs.

"Why did you do all of this, Emrys?"

He presses his forehead to mine.

"To prove to you that I meant what I said. You are important to me—you are the only thing that truly matters. If you choose me, this can be our life together. Whatever you want, I'll make it yours without hesitation."

"And if the time came when I wanted to leave, would you still permit me to go?"

I don't know why I ask. Perhaps it is the last tendril of self-preservation moving my lips.

Emrys pulls back slightly and averts my gaze.

"I won't lie to you, my blossom. After spending this time with you, it would be...difficult to let you go. Unbearable even. I would do anything in my power to persuade you to stay. Use tactics I wouldn't be proud of to keep you with me."

I hold my breath as his dark eyes return to mine.

"But," he says softly, "even as much as I want to, I could never keep you caged. Not even if it was in a gilded one by my side. That's why I would only ask you to make me one promise in exchange for your release."

"What kind of promise?" I ask. His lips are close enough to feel his soft breath.

"Promise me you'll never return to your family."

I raise a brow as he continues.

"I've glimpsed your spirit, Laurelle—your soul. It is too beautiful to be stifled by societal rules. If you grow to desire a human life, I want you to be free. No matter what you choose, I demand that you never hide yourself again."

Water pools in my eyes and slides down my cheeks. I don't give myself a chance to think. His words threaded through my heart; like a puppet, they yank me towards him. Gripping his head, I pull his face towards mine and slam my lips onto his.

They are motionless for a moment, my brain trying to warn me that we're making a mistake, but I don't listen. I just feel. Emrys realizes I'm kissing him in an instant and lets out a strangled growl. It echoes down my throat and into my racing heart.

His lips are feverish against mine. I've only kissed one other person, and that was years ago. If my technique is bad, the king surely does not notice. I whimper against his soft lips as we turn into a frenzy of touches and clashing teeth. His taste is crisp and sweet. Perfect. He tastes like forever.

Who needs faerie wine when his lips make me feel like this?

I don't want to stop, but I have to breathe and tell my faerie king my truth. All of it.

"I want to stay," I whisper against his mouth. "My heart knows we belong together. My soul demands yours, and I want to be with you."

I barely get the words out before his mouth is back on mine. Our mouths feast on each other as if we can devour the other. My hands leave his neck and slide down his naked back, sliding along the strong planes of muscles. I dig into his shoulder blades and moan.

With my mouth open, Emrys seizes the chance to

plunge his tongue into my mouth. It dances with my own—tasting and taking all that it can. We kiss as if we are fighting for dominance. It is delicious chaos, and I want more of it. I'll never get enough of this feeling—of him.

I need more. Now.

My hands drop from his back and go to the top of my dress. I manage to slip one sleeve off before Emrys stills my hands. Growling my own protest against his mouth, my eyes pop open.

"Not yet." His kiss is searing, even as he slips my sleeve back on me. "One more surprise, my blossom."

"Your cock can be the surprise," I whine, trying to pull his mouth back to mine.

He laughs before giving me another hot kiss.

"I won't let my need to fuck you stop me from spoiling you utterly rotten." Another hot kiss makes my lips tingle. "Or giving you the truth."

His lips press against my cheek. Softly, he kisses under my ear before gently nipping at my lobe. I gasp, my pussy turning even wetter. My thighs are surely soaked. His lips trail down my neck, biting and sucking as he goes. Claws skim down my sides until they tangle at my hips.

"But I am not a cruel king," he whispers before nipping under my chin. "I'll take the edge off for you."

With a gentle push, I fall backward onto one of the tables we had used to make the pies. I land with a gentle thud. Together, we push bowls and pans out of the way and listen to them clatter to the tile floor. I don't care if we're ruining all these beautiful pies. I need Emrys to touch me again. I need to feel him, or I'm going to die.

A bowl of jelly splatters to the floor, and I pay it no mind. Just like I pay no mind to the flour coating my hair and dress as I reach down and yank up my skirts. Emrys's claws tangle with mine until my pussy is completely exposed to his greedy eyes and the evening air.

"So pretty." Emrys trails a claw up my wet slit, eliciting a moan from me.

"Emrys," I whine. Opening my legs wider, I watch as he tosses them over his shoulder and grips my hips. Yanking me towards his face, he inhales against my wet flesh as my hands tangle in his white hair.

"This perfect pussy needs to be worshipped." He inhales deeply once more. "It needs to be kept safe at all times. It's the ultimate treasure—one humans were never fit to behold."

His tongue licks up my center, and I scream. I'm already dangerously close to climax. I always am whenever he touches me. My back arches, and a cloud of flour coats the air around us.

"Look at how wet you are, Laurelle. You're soaking the table."

With his tongue returning to my clit, I feel his claw circle my entrance before gently pushing inside. The stretch is decadent, and my moans become louder. My chest rises and falls as he pumps me with his finger. Closing his lips around my clit, he sucks gently, and I scream out his name.

My body is teetering on the edge when I feel him pull his finger from me. New heat pools in my belly as I feel him skim that same claw down between the cheeks of my ass. My face flames as he gently prods my back entrance, as his tongue spears into my pussy.

"Emrys!" My hands tighten in his hair.

"Before the night is over," he growls against me, "you'll beg me to be in both of your little holes. In your mouth. You'll demand my cock fill you with seed everywhere it can."

"Yes," I agree, lost to my pleasure.

"I can see it now, my blossom. You spread out before me like this. So sweet and tempting. Your body is covered in my bites. My back is red from your nails gripping me."

He sucks my clit again as he pushes his finger all the way into my ass. My scream echoes around the room. The heat from the ovens causes my body to break out into a fine sheen of sweat. My hair clings to my temples.

"You know what else I'm going to see, my love?"

My heart catches at the term of endearment, but I manage to ask, "What else?"

"I'm going to see my seed seeping out from your sweet pussy. I'll see some of it dried along your breasts. And the corner of your mouth. But it's your pussy that will be over-flowing with it. Filled to the point that it will seep out and soak the sheets of our bed. Isn't that what you want?"

I nod my head, the muscles in my body tightening.

"And you know what you'll say to me?"

"What?"

His breath hovers over my clit, and I feel him smile against me.

"You'll beg me to use my seed to fuck your ass. To stretch you open and flood you with my come there. It'll hurt, but you'll love it."

Clamping his lips over my clit once more, he shoves a second finger into my back entrance, and my body erupts. Molten glass seeps through my veins as my thighs tighten around his head. The hard twigs of his crown dig into my thighs as I thrash through my orgasm.

My pussy clamps around nothing as I rock my hips against his face.

Emrys never falters as he sees me through every second of it. He pulls his fingers from me and licks me clean. His tongue tastes every inch of me until my hips lower back down to the workbench. He doesn't stop, even as I shake through the final waves of my orgasm.

My eyes are heavy as I watch him spread me wide and feast on me again. I shiver—my body is too sensitive from the intense climax.

His dark eyes find mine as he lowers my legs from his shoulders and pulls my skirts from my waist. Gently, he pulls me up before kissing me softly. My taste mingles with his. His hands brush through my curls as he holds my body tight to his.

Lifting me in his strong arms, he cradles me to his chest as we exit the kitchen. Walking us down the hall, my breath is still shallow, and my body feels utterly relaxed.

We must've gotten truly carried away in the kitchen because when we emerged outside, the sky is already an inky black. The stars above twinkle down at us, and a cool breeze tugs at my dress. It feels nice on my warm skin.

Emrys takes us through the meadow until we are once again at the clearing from last night. A silk sheet is laid out, and the sprites and faeries hug the tree-line. Gently, Emrys sets me down on the covered ground before sitting behind me. My back rests against his chest, and his hands hold me to him.

The sprites float towards us and illuminate the space with their glowing bodies. My head falls back against Emrys's shoulder as I absorb his closeness. Raising a hand, Emrys directs my attention to the night sky.

"Watch," he whispers in my ear.

As if they are alive, the stars begin to move. They swirl around in a dazzling circle. My breath hitches as they cut through the sky like water. Such beautiful magic.

The stars slow their movements until they form a massive tree. Its trunk is tall, and its branches are far-reaching. The stars file in on each other to create the great mass of leaves.

"Long ago, there was *The Great Oak,* and from it sprouted all faerie life," Emrys explains, his voice clear and strong.

I watch as a new scene is illustrated by the sparkling embers. They form the bodies of sprites—buzzing around and wreaking havoc. The scene transforms into the meadow, but one that is trampled and unorganized. A far cry from what it is now.

"But *The Great Oak* knew that they could not be left to their own devices. They needed a ruler to keep this realm in order," Emrys continues.

I watch the scene in the sky change again, and the massive tree is once more illuminated. From its strong truck, a cluster of stars breaks off and swirl into a familiar figure.

"From it's magical bark, I was born. The faerie king. Given my power from *The Great Oak* to control the meadow and maintain order."

Emrys's handsome face is cast in glowing stars and my heart speeds up.

"But *The Great Oak* had a secret." The scene changes once more into the tree. I watch in silent shock as golden stars fall from the branches and fade to nothing before reaching the bottom of the thick trunk. "It was dying, and with it, so would the meadow and all who inhabited it."

I open my mouth to say something—the sprites around me pale and hang their heads. Even Emrys's clear voice has become tinged with sadness. The truth of what he's explaining to me spears into my heart. My hand grips his as I turn to face him.

"Unless the prophecy could be fulfilled," he says softly, his hand cupping my cheek.

Gently, he tips my face back up to the sky and I gasp. It's

Emrys and I, made out of glowing stars. Hand in hand, we walk towards *The Great Oak* and slip inside. The stars twist and shift, and the scene becomes more erotic. We are both naked—our bodies moving with each other while the tree around us glows brighter.

"As the prophecy goes, the king must take a human into the heart of *The Great Oak* and claim her. To restore its power by infusing his back into it. Only then could *The Great Oak* be revived by the offering of two souls and the primal magic that is made when they fuse together."

The stars glow bright once more before spreading out. The story ends, and they resume their typical place in the sky. Turning back towards Emrys, my eyes search his. Raising his hand, I notice a laurel of wildflowers. They are a riot of colors—blues, oranges, pinks, and whites—and smell delicious. Emrys smiles as he sets it on my head.

"The prophecy," I whisper.

I feel the flower crown settle there. With a gentle tug, the crown does not budge from its place on my head. Power flows through me and feels like Emrys—exciting and heady. It's not painful. It feels right. Permanent. As if I've always belonged here and always will.

"I've waited a long time for you, my blossom. All of my realm has, but they will continue to wait until you are ready. I won't complete this prophecy without you. It is you who hold the power," he whispers.

I lick my lips. "You've never taken anyone inside *The Great Oak*?"

He shakes his head. "Never."

"And you want to take me?"

"More than anything," he confesses. "You're the most beautiful woman I've ever seen. I want to own and keep you. I want to possess you. Laying claim to your soul during the ritual will be the greatest honor and the most wonderful pleasure. I want nothing more than to bind your soul to mine because you've owned me since the moment I saw you."

I stare into his earnest eyes. I can feel the sprites and faeries humming around us—willing us together. Who am I to deny them? I want to keep this realm safe, but more than that, I want Emrys. I want his kindness—his devotion and desire. He's given me my freedom and stoked my pleasure, and now I'm ready. To be a permanent fixture of this land and to do it by his side.

If I've owned his soul since the moment we met, then he most assuredly has owned mine.

My mind whispers that this has to be some sort of trick, but that voice sounds an awful lot like my mother and father's. I shake myself gently. No more will I think of them. No more will I let myself be ruled by their expectations and rules. I will be just as free as my king demands me to be.

The king who I love.

The realization makes the silence between us stretch. I love him. I do. It's too fast, but it's true. I should tell him, but not yet. First, I want to show him what he means to me— what he'll always mean to me.

Winding my hands through his soft hair, I twist until I'm straddling his lap. My legs lock around his back as I bring our mouths together. The kiss is soft and claiming. It's the first one of the rest of our lives together. Pulling back slightly, I touch our foreheads together.

"Take me to *The Great Oak*."

10

LAURELLE

Emrys carries me like I'm made of delicate glass.

His steps are quick and sure as we pass through rows of sweet-smelling flowers. Sprites fly up around us—cheering and offering congratulations. A few faeries throw white petals that cling to our knees. I'd say they seem more excited than me, but that would be a lie. My body hums with anticipation.

We cut through a row of thick trees beyond Emrys's palace. A few leaves tickle my cheeks, but Emrys's hold stays locked on me. I snuggle into his warm chest. Any nerves I have fade, and only eagerness swirls in my stomach.

Soon, I will have him, and soon we will be one.

While the prophecy is important, it isn't the only factor driving me and Emrys together. I want and care for him, and because of that, I want to help him save this beautiful, magical realm. The fact that he's never taken anyone else in here tells me all I need to know. If his depth of feeling for me wasn't clear before, it surely is now.

Pushing through the dense foliage, we emerge in a moonlit clearing. It's easily triple the size of the one the faeries and I danced through a few nights ago. This one is sequestered away, hidden to conceal an ancient secret. The sprites fly towards it and lounge on the branches of the surrounding trees.

A new sensation tickles my body. It pulses with energy— a different sort of magic zips through the air. A dense fog obscures the center. The damp wind tugs at my thin dress. Still, Emrys presses on until the cloudy air recedes, and my breath stills in my lungs.

It's magnificent. Even compared to all the things I've seen, *The Great Oak* is beyond compare.

Glowing with a pure golden light, the massive tree reaches into the sky at a shocking height. It's made up of hundreds of strong branches—all of them decorated in golden leaves. It feels warm despite the cool evening air. Its trunk is wider than a castle wall. Sprites and faeries swarm it, allowing their glowing bodies to add even more light to its impressive structure.

My eyes snag on a few bare branches, and my heart dips.

Emrys raises a hand at the tree, and the trunk gently peels open. Its golden bark folds in on its side. A gentle, crunching sound fills the clearing until there is a hole big enough for the two of us to step through.

Emrys takes us through the opening as I stare at my surroundings. The walls and floor are bare oak wood. Inside glows from an unknown light source. Magic, I assume. A few windows are carved along the oak walls of the room. They peer out into the dark night sky.

I'd expected the inside to be more similar to Emrys's palace—a tree that opens into a swath of rooms—however, we seem to be in a sort of wooden pocket. It is just one simple room carved into this wide trunk. Simple, its purpose clear, and my face warms.

Emrys gently sets me on my feet, and I sag back against his chest.

He says nothing as he takes my hand and raises it up before us. A slight sting tickles my palm, and I watch in shock as the empty space before us is covered in fine silks and over-stuffed pillows. There's a thick mattress that looks akin to a cloud. The fabrics sparkle in the light, and I know in my heart that I've summoned these things.

I have magic—somehow. Part of me wishes to explore this newfound power, but as I watch the final pillows land softly on the bed, I only care about being with my king.

As if sensing my thoughts, Emrys collects me at my waist and deposits me on the bed. Despite the open windows, the inside of the tree is pleasantly warm. The floors and walls seem to pulse with life as if we are inside something living.

Emrys stands before me, his eyes dark and hot. We gaze at each other—our desire stealing our words. His hands skim up my sides, and I let out a soft sigh. My own hands curl behind his neck and yank his face down to mine.

Our lips connect, and the tree around us blazes in a new wave of golden light. My eyes pop open to see what just our simple touch has done. His lips on mine never waver, and I let myself be overwhelmed by his delicious taste.

There is power in here—heady and all-consuming— and I'm happily giving myself over to it.

Pulling him fully on top of me, I shimmy up the bed until he falls between my splayed thighs. Our mouths collide in a frenzy of kisses and bites as our hands tangle together. This kiss is a glimpse, a taste, of our future together. I moan as I swallow it down.

His tongue dances with mine as his claws shred my gown, leaving my hot skin exposed to the room.

Breaking for air, Emrys stares down at my naked body.

His claws close over one of my breasts and give it a gentle squeeze. My eyes are heavy as I feel the soft skin of his sides slide against my inner thighs.

"I don't know what to do," I whisper. "How am I supposed to perform this ritual?"

Emry's smile is all teeth.

"By letting me pleasure you, my blossom. That's all *The Great Oak* demands of us. Look at what we've already done."

Indeed, the room glows with more golden light. The tree pulses with fresh power and Emrys has barely even touched me.

His lips return to mine, and I tangle my hands in his silk hair. His tongue tastes my lips before gently biting down on my lower lip. The little nip of pain has more wetness slicking out of me. I have to be soaking the silk below us.

Emrys's mouth traces down my neck. Biting and sucking as he goes, and my toes curl into the sheets. We've done this before, and yet it feels like the first time. It's familiar yet foreign.

Laying open-mouth kisses along my chest, he gently squeezes my right breast before his tongue swirls around my other nipple. I moan as he sucks it fully into his mouth, rolling the hard bud between his teeth. I'm panting as I watch him give my other breast the same treatment.

My body is on fire, and he's only adding more fuel to it.

His claws skim up the sensitive skin of my thighs before reaching my pussy. I gasp as his claw parts my soaked flesh and gently enters me. My eyes flutter close at the sensation. He's gentle as he fills me, pumping his finger slowly until my teeth clench. Carefully, he works another finger inside of me, the stretch decadent.

He's preparing me for his cock, and that realization makes more arousal surge from me. It seeps down my thighs, and I can hear the sloppy, wet sounds his fingers are making as they pump me. Emrys nips the fleshy swell of my breast, and my eyes pop open.

Black eyes sear into my soul.

"Are you going to be a good girl, Laurelle?" he asks. My reply is a moan as he works a third finger into me. "Are you going to let me put my cock in this tight little pussy?"

His fingers still deep inside me. I try to move my hips to get some friction, but his claws pin my hips to the bed.

"Yes!" I cry out. A smile curves his lips as his fingers curl inside me. They brush up against a spot deep inside me, and my stomach clenches. Pleasure sings down my spine, and my groans become more unabashed.

"Even if it hurts?" he asks. "If only for a moment?"

Words escape me as I nod my head. My eyes threaten to close at this new onslaught of pleasure. I'm close, and I feel my thighs tremble along the sides of his hips.

Using his grip on my hips to leverage me, Emrys pushes me further onto my back until my hips tip up. This exposed, I can fully see his fingers—pale green and tipped in black— disappearing into my soaked pussy. Wetness shines on the inside of my thighs. My legs threaten to close, but he hooks his hand under my left knee and keeps them open.

Being this exposed, I wait for shyness or shame to steal my pleasure, but it doesn't. I want him to see me like this— to know that all of this is because of him.

"Use your words, my blossom," my faerie king growls.

"I want—I want—"

Words are hard when his fingers are fucking me this good. They work that secretive spot inside of me over and over again until my peak is just within reach.

Then his hand stills once more, and I let out a frustrated growl. My eyes blaze fury into his. Emrys merely smirks.

"Tell me what you want, and I'll continue."

"I..." With my pleasure so close, I let the truth of my heart spill free. There's no reason to hide anymore. There never was any reason. "I want you fuck me. Make me come—first with your fingers so I can lick them clean. Then I want your cock inside of me. Stretching me and filling me with your seed until it seeps out of me for hours, like you promised. I want to feel you every time I move tomorrow."

His fingers hook inside of me as he growls.

"Be my first," I cry, pleasure barreling towards me. "Be my only."

A warm, wet tongue licks my clit, and my whole body erupts. I arch clear off the bed, my muscles clamping so tight around his fingers that I fear I may break them.

I feel my come seep from me and soak his hand as he continues to pump me through my climax. It soaks my thighs—the smattering of curls covering my pussy. Still, my king doesn't stop as he wrings more pleasure from my body.

My muscles were tight, and now they are decadently languid. I feel like I am floating. Aftershocks of pleasure make me shiver and gasp. Faintly, I am aware of Emrys pulling his fingers from me. I open my heavy eyes to meet his gaze.

It's filled with affection and lust. He extends his hand towards my mouth and smears my release on my lips and chin. Clasping his large hand in mine, I suck his finger into my mouth. I taste myself and his skin. Moaning around his finger, I gently nip at the tip of his claw.

His eyes grow wide as he growls.

"Such a good girl," he praises. "Suck me. Taste yourself and understand the delicious treat you are."

I feel him shift between my thighs as I move on to the

next finger. Emrys tosses something behind him, and I realize a moment too late it's his pants.

His finger leaves my mouth with a pop as I feel his cock push into my entrance. The tip is round and smooth. Glancing down, I get my first real look at his cock, and *Great Oak spare me...*

It's massive. Slightly darker green than the rest of his skin. Thick and already dripping with milky white seed at the tip. That wetness, mixed with my own, helps him glide just past my entrance. He's barely inside of me, and I already feel full. His hand traces down my chest, giving my breast a gentle squeeze before cupping my hip.

"Are you ready for me?" His voice is barely audible.

I nod my head as he shifts his hips slightly forward. The stretch and burn are great. I force my eyes to stay open as I watch his thick shaft part of my wet flesh. He's not even halfway in. His cock is a blessing—and also my greatest adversary.

"Words, Laurelle. I need the words."

Pressing up on my heels, I slip more of him inside of me with a strangled moan. My hands find the muscular curves of his backside and give a gentle pull.

"Take me. I was born to serve only you. A vessel for your pleasure."

With a strangled groan, Emrys goes to slide inside me more, but I'm impatient. Using what little strength I have left, I haul him the rest of the way inside of me. There is a pinch of pain—the feel of him stretching me is not without discomfort. Yet, I don't shift away. If anything, I drag him closer until our chests are pressed together. Opening my legs wider, I let his hips become flush with mine.

His breathing is ragged as he stays still inside of me, allowing me to adjust to his great length. My hands skim up his back and tangle in his hair. Emrys lays kisses on my fore-head. His lips press against the tip of my nose before working their way down my neck. His deep voice murmurs praise with each kiss.

"Beautiful," he whispers. "Perfect. Your cunt was made for me. Tell me you're okay, my blossom."

His eyes find mine—concerned etched on his face. I cup his cheek and give him a gentle smile. Our lips press together, and my heart overflows with emotion. This is perfect. It's beyond anything that I could've ever imagined. Those old novels I used to read are nothing compared to this. The feeling of him inside me is beyond words.

And I want more.

Looking him in the eye, I break our kiss and say against his mouth, "Fuck me."

The command is simple, but it unleashes my faerie king.

His hips pull back before thrusting inside of me. The force is strong enough to have my breasts jolting. His hard cock fills me completely and presses up against my womb. He's so deep and wide, and if there was any question that I was meant for him, they're quickly done away with. I shouldn't be able to take him like this, but I can't get enough.

As if we were truly crafted to become one.

"Yes!" I scream as he thrusts into me again. "I have to have this forever. I can't live without it—without you."

"I'll never deny you a thing."

He pulls out of me until only the head of his massive cock remains inside me. My moan catches in my throat as he tosses my legs over his shoulder and shifts our angle. When he pushes inside me again, it will be even deeper, and anticipation tightens my muscles.

"You're too tight, too perfect."

"Impossible," I whine, trying to sheath more of him inside of me. "Please, *please*, give me your cock. Don't deny me the one thing I want the most."

With a strangled groan, he plunges deep inside of me. My hands cover his as he holds onto my hips. The sharp pricks of his claws only heighten my pleasure. I hope they leave behind a mark.

Mercilessly, he fucks me. His thrusts are hard yet gentle. Our bodies slap together in a symphony of sweaty, sticky skin. It's indecent, and it's exactly as it should be. I feel our hearts beating in time—our souls being threaded together. His earthy scent overwhelms me, and I taste it in the air.

"Look at how greedy you are for my cock," he says. "This little cunt is soaking me. It knows who's laid claim to her. Who owns her for the rest of eternity."

"It's yours. Just as I am," I pant.

"Greedy girl. A human man could never have given you this. Isn't that right?"

"Never!"

"Only me. Only this cock can truly satisfy such a sweet pussy."

His hips smack into my ass, causing my body to slide up the bed. My hands sink into the silk sheets and curl into fists. My moans are sloppy and loud. Lifting my legs from his shoulders, he folds them together before twisting my bottom half onto its side. Sliding into me once more is deep and tight. My king easily steals my breath.

"Emrys," I moan, my muscles tightening once more.

My eyes find the open window and gasp as I take in the glowing bodies there. The faeries and sprites watch through unblinking eyes. They lounge on the open window and float on their gossamer wings.

Emrys thrusts into me, and a moan slips past my lips.

The sprites cheer in a flurry of glowing bodies. Should I be embarrassed that they're watching? I'm not. In fact, I enjoy their eyes. After having to hide myself for so long, claiming my desire and freedom so openly heightens my pleasure.

My faerie king cups my knees and pulls them open. Our hips meet as he fucks me over and over again. His mouth lands on mine as he tastes and teases. His claws roll and pinch my nipples.

"Do you enjoy them watching?" he asks. My cheeks warm, and I nod.

His hand travels between my legs as he traces the tip of his claw around my clit. He smirks and shakes his head.

"Only naughty girls are so wanton in public."

Pleasure calls to me. My peak is so close I can taste it.

"I want to be naughty," I admit. "Only with you."

His smile is pure male confidence as his mouth meets mine again. His tongue licks over my lips. I open my mouth to let him in as he slams his thick length into me over and over again. With each thrust, he claims a piece of my soul for himself.

Pulling back from me, Emrys says, "They want to watch the completion of the ritual. Should we allow them?"

Biting my lip, I nod my head. Golden light pours from between our connected bodies. *The Great Oak* seems to swell with each slap of our flesh.

Quick as lightning, Emrys shifts our positions once more. I protest as he pulls out of me, and my back lands against his chest. With his legs hanging off the edge of the mattress, he lifts me onto his lap. My knees rest on either side of his thighs.

His claws grip my chin and tip my face forward. My heart races as I watch the glowing figures fill the entryway and windows. Their eyes stare at us—rapt and undivided.

"Give them a good show, my blossom," Emrys urges.

With a shaky moan, I reach below and find his hard cock. I run my hand through my come coating him, and give him a gentle tug. He hisses as he pushes my curls off my sweaty back. His tongue licks up my spine as I press up on my knees. I work him around my entrance before sheathing the tip inside of me.

"Oh, Emrys," I moan, sliding down his impressive length. This way is obscenely decadent. The stretch is otherworldly. I rise up on my knees before sinking fully onto him again.

The sprites and faeries before us cheer and dance. Their bodies hum and glow anew, just as *The Great Oak* does. Emrys's hand comes to my hip and helps raise and lower me on his hardness. Over and over again, I take his length as my moan ratchet up.

"Once my seed spills inside of you, the ritual will be complete. *The Great Oak's* power will be restored, and you will be queen. You already wear the crown."

My hand comes up to the flowers woven through my hair. They pulse under my fingers. I feel powerful, as if each thrust is infusing me with more and more magic. It feels permanent claiming. Just as permanent as my love for Emrys.

"Come. Inside. Me." I bite out each word on a thrust. "Fill me with your seed. I need my king's come."

Emrys growls, his claws tightening on me as he pulls me off his length and throws me face down at the end of the bed.

"Then you shall have it," he growls against my ear.

He thrusts into me with one powerful stroke, and my chest knocks to the bed. He yanks my hips upward, and my fingers find the sheets. His hands are the only thing holding me up as he pounds me into the mattress. Each thrust jolts me forward and pulls my climax towards me.

Flames lick my skin, and my muscles begin to tremble.

The sprites buzz around us. A few faeries have even ventured into the room, their small footsteps barely audible. Those in the crowd mirror the sound of our skin smacking —clearly more than eager to participate in their own wanton display. My moans are choppy as he ruts into me.

His claw skims between the cheeks of my ass, and I feel him press at the tight ring of muscle back there.

"Hear me, my blossom. We won't leave this oak until I've claimed all your little holes. I already promised as much."

His thumb breaches my back entrance, and it sets off my release. When his other hand rubs my clit, I'm done for. I scream into the sheets, my whole body shaking as my come drips out of me and covers him. My muscles clamp down around his hard length, and I feel our connection between my legs and in my heart.

Emrys thrusts hard into me once, twice, and on the third, he lets out a guttural growl before his warmth soaks me. He comes and comes until I feel his seed mingling with my own and sliding down my thighs. I feel a strange tightening in my chest as it flows into me.

Looking up, the room blazes with golden light—brighter than the sun. Fresh flowers sprout up between my fingers from where my hands grip the bed. A harsh wind blows through *The Great Oak*, pushing the sprites and faeries from the room. They let out a scream as they land outside. A metallic taste coats my tongue at the abundance of fresh magic.

My body still shakes with my orgasm as Emrys embeds his teeth in my shoulder. The bite is harsh and claiming, and it sets off another climax as I feel our hearts and souls become one. Two halves finally becoming whole.

The sprites cheer and titter outside as Emrys jerks one last time inside me.

Glancing over my shoulder, my eyes can barely stay open. I watch as Emrys kisses the bite on my shoulder before gently pulling out of me. My curls cling to my sweaty temples, and I try my best to tuck some behind my ear.

Emrys's hands grip my side and gently pull me down to the bed on top of his chest. My hand lands over his heart, and I feel it racing under my palm. Even Emrys seems to glow. He hums with new power. His crown is dotted with fresh golden leaves. My own skin seems to be sparkling as if my blood flows gold instead of red.

I'm too tired to take it all in.

With a deep sigh, I snuggle into his chest and let our mingling releases dry on my thighs. I love the feeling of him seeping out of me. I love the claim.

My eyes are already closing when Emrys's claws skim down my cheek.

"Are you okay?" he whispers.

Sleep has stolen my voice, but I manage to open my eyes and smile. Giving him a small nod, he gathers me tighter against his chest. His lips brush mine, and it takes everything I have to return it.

"Sleep, my blossom," he commands. "I'll have my cock in you again soon enough."

Despite my exhaustion I manage to giggle and find my voice.

"Can't wait," I slur before drifting into a deep, boneless sleep.

Even in sleep, she is perfect.

Her gorgeous face is relaxed—her whole body is warm and trusting in my arms. I should be sleeping as well, but I can't. Not as our lovemaking still pumps through my veins and *The Great Oak* hums around us with new magic.

The prophecy has been fulfilled. Satisfaction should be coursing through me, and in truth, I am happy that my realm is no longer in danger. But satisfied? I can't say that I am anything but restless as a new hunger burrows under my skin.

This new need roars in my veins, demanding I claim my blossom over and over again. To be awake and not inside her is torture. To not hear her call my name as she comes is an unbearably cruel punishment.

At least I have my eyes on her. Even watching her, helps some of the sharpest parts of my desire dull. I'll guard her as she sleeps. I'll wait for her to be ready for me again, and I'll enjoy the warmth of her embrace and siphon as much pleasure from her as I can before she needs to rest once more.

My whole kingdom is asleep. The excitement of tonight taking its toll on everyone.

Even though my body is exhausted, my heart and mind are alert. Need, raw and hot, pulses through me. I try and quiet my mind by counting Laurelle's freckles. I've just gotten to number seventy-two when she stirs against my chest.

Her plumb lips part with a sigh as she burrows closer to me. Pride and primal urges dance in my chest. My claws skim up her back and over her delicate shoulder eliciting a small shiver from her. Tracing up her throat, I swallow my growl at my claiming bite. The imprint of my teeth is an unwavering indication of who owns her.

My cock hardens at the sight.

Continuing their exploration, my hands skim back down the soft skin of her back. How can someone be this perfect? This delicate? Her shame and shyness are gone. Eradicated by my touch and I revel in it. I laid claim to her soul—her heart—and I will keep them safe for all eternity.

My claws dig into the fleshy swell of her ass, and Laurelle shifts closer. Her warm breath bathes my throat as her brown, gold-flecked eyes blink open at me. They glow with the magic we created here. The magic that belongs to her and makes her brown skin glow.

Her lips curve into a soft smile. Affection warms her gaze.

A queen is what she is. My queen.

"Why aren't you sleeping?" Her voice is rough as she cups my cheek. Her thumb gently traces the line of my cheekbone.

"I enjoy watching you too much to rest."

She laughs, slinging her leg further over my hips and snuggling closer to me. I can feel my dried seed on her leg, and my thoughts turn wicked. I send up a prayer of thanks to *The Great Oak* for putting Laurelle in my path. She's too perfect for me and I will spend the rest of our lives proving myself worthy of having such a gift as her.

"You're not tired?" Her voice vibrates against my neck.

"Not tired enough to take my eyes off you."

She shakes her head, her curls tickling my cheeks. Rising up slightly on her arms, her naked breasts come into view, and my blood heats. Perfect. They filled my hands as if molded for them, and I long to taste them once more.

A grin curves her lips as if she knows what I'm thinking. Clearly, she felt my cock stir to life once more. My hand runs up her neck and tangle in her hair. I let her curls slip through my fingers before reaching her flower crown.

It's beautiful, made of flowers just as wild as her. Nothing is more befitting of my lovely queen. It's more than an accessory; it shows her permanent place at my side. We will rule this land together, hand in hand, and I will worship her every day of our reign.

"I don't know how you aren't sleepy," she whispers, her hand tracing the muscles of my chest. Biting her lower lip, her face is the picture of innocence. "Maybe you need some help relaxing?"

I get her meaning when her curious hand travels down my stomach. My whole body tights as she wraps her small hand around my cock. It's already hard and dripping. Even that small touch has seed spilling from the tip.

Knocking back the silk sheets, I expose our naked bodies to the room. Laurelle moans as she glances between us. Her hand barely wraps around my length as she gives me a gentle squeeze. I hiss, and she moans in answer.

Despite loving her touch more than anything, I can't help but check in on her.

"You don't have to do this, Laurelle." My claws dig into her waist. "I know you're exhausted. Sleep. My cock will still be hard when you wake. That I promise you."

Instead of releasing me, she gives another tight pump of her fist, and I groan. Wickedness gleams in her brown eyes as she rolls on top of me. Her lips press against mine, and I cup her head. I'm lost to her sweet mouth. Her small hand pumps my cock in time with her thrusting tongue. It makes my head spin.

We're both breathless as we pull apart. My shaft is trapped between my abs and her soft stomach. Pressing our foreheads together, Laurelle smirks at me. A powerful queen merely toying with her willing subject.

"You said we weren't leaving until you claimed all my holes," I growl as she places a soft kiss on my chest. "I woke up with this craving, my king. Shall I tell you about it?"

"Yes," I growl as she licks over one of my nipples. My wild and wanton Laurelle. "I command you, reveal all your desires."

She bites her lip as she stares up at me.

"Your taste," she whispers. "I dreamed of what you would taste like. Of what your hard cock sliding against my tongue would feel like. Would you deny me?"

"Never." My growl rattles the room.

"Good."

Her mouth kisses down my chest. She bites and sucks as she goes and now I bare her markings. Pride warms my chest. My Laurelle is possessive and I'm more than happy to be claimed by her.

I spread my legs wider to accommodate her between them. My cock hardens further until it stands proud—preening for her attention. Her eyes are wide as she realizes just what was inside her from earlier. And what will soon be filling her perfect mouth.

She gives me another tug before tucking her dark curls behind her ear. Bracing her hand on my thigh, her delicious breasts graze me as her pink tongue tentatively licks the bead of seed at the tip. Moaning, she swallows it down.

Hazy eyes lock with mine.

"You lie, my king," she states.

"About what?" My heart races. She licks up the length of my shaft.

"You said there was nothing sweeter than my pussy, but...have you never tasted yourself?"

"Laurelle," I growl. Her lips curve into a wide smile before she leans down again.

Wrapping her perfect lips around the head of my cock, she sucks me deeper into her mouth. It's warm and wet and Laurelle. The only thing more decadent than her mouth is her sweet pussy. Her head bobs in time with her fist as she jerks me. Her saliva coats my shaft and wet, smacking sounds fill the room.

Deeper and deeper she takes me into her mouth until I'm in her throat. She chokes once, twice, as if testing her limits. My hands tangle in her hair and lift her face towards mine. Saliva coats her lips and dribbles down her chin. Her eyes water but I can smell her deepening scent.

She loves this almost as much as I do.

More seed seeps from my tip, and she eagerly licks it away.

"Cock-hungry little girl, aren't you?"

She nods her head, working me deeper into her throat once more.

"You look so pretty with my cock in your mouth."

Releasing my length with a pop, she gazes up at me.

"Am I doing alright? I've never done this before, but I've always wanted to."

I raise a brow as jealousy tightens my chest.

"Really? Did you think of doing this with a human man?"

Her eyes widen, and she shakes her head. "Never."

My jealousy dissipates as she continues.

"I only heard about this in passing from a few of our servants. I never thought it would appeal to me, yet when I met you, I wanted to try. To know what it would be like to taste you here. I—"

She pauses and looks away, her mouth going back to my cock. I capture her face before she can take me back inside her. I use my thumb to pull her pink lip down.

"Say the rest," I command. Her cheeks color, but she nods.

"I had this fantasy long, long ago. Something I read in a book my mother took from me. It's something I've been wanting for us to try."

"Tell me, and I'll make it yours."

My curiosity is peaked further as her cheeks fill with color and she bites her lip.

"I imagined you standing in front of me. My knees on the floor and my hands gripping your thighs." Her breath picks up, and I watch her squirm. "I thought of your claws pricking my scalp as you guide my mouth up and down your cock. I'd choke and spit, but I'd keep going as far as I could so that I could please you."

My balls draw up tight, and I'm dangerously close to spilling all over her delicate hand. Shuffling her back, I wait for her knees to hit the floor in front of the bed. Standing over her, I stare down into her face. With a wave of my hand, a couple of pillows stuff themselves under her knees so she doesn't hurt herself but also to make her the perfect height for what I plan to do.

Curling my claws into her hair, I let them press into her scalp and her mouth opens with a gasp. Seizing the opportunity, I rock my hips forward and sheath myself inside her warm mouth.

She groans, sending delicious vibrations down my cock. Her hands come up to my thighs before slipping around and gripping my ass. I thrust into her mouth over and over again. I slide against her wet tongue. I bump the back of her throat, and she gags. Tears stream down her golden brown cheeks as her eyes flame with more desire.

"Is this what you wanted? For me to fuck your face just like I did your little cunt?"

She makes a garbled sound, and I yank her off my length. Swallowing down her saliva, I revel in the beautiful mess I've made of her.

"Use your words," I command.

"Yes," she gasps. "Just like this. I love it."

"Good girl. Such a naughty little cock-slut you are."

She gasps at my words. They would've offended the old Laurelle, but this one lets them wash over her. My queen is a dirty girl who likes cock in her mouth and my fingers in her ass. She wants to be taken roughly and crudely by someone she trusts.

And I'm the lucky creature who gets to have her.

"Tell me you love being my little fuck-toy," I command.

She squeezes my ass, and I can hear her come soaking the floor beneath her. I'll lick it up later.

"I love it," she says.

"Tell me you want me to come in your pretty little throat."

"Please, come in my mouth, Emrys. I crave your taste."

"I'll feed you this cock every night. You won't even need food. This will keep you fulfilled for eternity."

She garbles her agreement before taking me back into her mouth. My grip on her head tightens as I rock against her warm tongue. She sucks and slurps me. Her mouth is tight and hot, and my spine is already beginning to tingle.

Her curious hand leaves my ass to graze under my shaft, and I'm done for. My roar scatters the birds lounging in *The Great Oak's* branches. My spine locks up, and my muscles tighten as the seed is ripped from me. Warmth spreads throughout my stomach as my teeth clench.

"Swallow it. Be a good girl."

Laurelle eagerly takes my come into her mouth. She gulps down two mouthfuls before I pull her from my length. Gripping my seeping cock, I line it up with her face.

The first spray of my seed covers her lips and chin. Her eyes widen as the next spray lands on her chest and drips down her breasts. I bathe her lips in my seed once more before shoving it back into her mouth.

Now sticky with my release, she cleans off my cock with efficiency.

Once my climax passes, I fall from her mouth once more. She licks over her lips and moans at my taste lingering there. My seed is smeared all over her perfect face and it's more decadent than I can bear.

Her thighs rub together, her floral scent drowning me. She looks up at me, a silent plea in her eyes.

"I know just what you need."

Plucking her from the ground, I toss her into the center of the bed. My face comes down between her splayed thighs, and I devour her wet flesh. It's soft and soaking wet. I rub my nose back and forth against her clit before sucking it into my mouth.

Her hands grip my head as she thrashes on the bed. The sheets around us are in tatters. Laurelle is lost to pleasure as she raises her hips against my tongue. She grinds against my face, demanding her orgasm.

My tongue spears into her entrance, and I taste our mingling releases. I groan as I lick her clean. Rubbing her clit with my thumb, her body locks. Those inner muscles clamp around my tongue as more wetness floods my mouth.

I drink her pleasure, swallowing her down just as she did for me. Her body shakes through it all. Her eyes are wide open, and her mouth is parted on a silent scream.

Slowly, her thighs loosen from my head. I expect her to pass out, but she doesn't. Her hands find my head, and she tilts my face towards her.

She's all queenly power when she demands, "Inside me."

I grin before pressing a soft kiss to her inner thigh.

Without giving her a warning, I cup her hips and flip her onto her stomach. Dragging her by the middle, I prop her up on her elbows and tip her hips up to face me. My claws dig into her ass and spread her cheeks wide. Both of her little holes are ripe for the taking.

"Emrys," she whines, not in embarrassment but in desire.

I spit down on her back entrance. Spearing my tongue into her ass as she squeals. Her muscles should be loose enough from the orgasm, but we'll still need to go slow. Incredibly slow as I ease a finger into her tight hole. I pump it inside of her slowly as she thrashes. I retreat the finger and plunge it back in, eliciting a scream from my blossom.

Perhaps I can't make good on my promise after all.

"You're too tight here," I explain. Gently, I withdraw my finger.

Her hand reaches back and captures mine. Looking over her shoulder, her eyes are firm.

"Fuck my ass."

"My blossom, I don't—"

"If it's too much, we'll stop, but I want to try." Her eyes implore me. "Please."

I growl. "You know I can't deny you when you use that word."

She giggles and props herself up on her elbows. Reaching down, I grip my cock, that's already hard, and begging to be back inside her any way it can. I press against her ass, and Laurelle moans.

Her smile is trusting as I gently push the tip inside of her.

Hot, tight muscles wrap around the head of my cock. It chokes the pleasure from me. Laurelle keens and claws at the bed. Gripping one of her cheeks, I hold her open. I have to see every moment of this.

I push in another inch, and her chest heaves. She's too perfect.

"I won't last longer than a minute," I confess. My seed is already embarrassingly close to spilling.

"Good," Laurelle groans.

I chuckle despite the onslaught of pleasure. My cock stretches her tight hole as I push as far in as I can. Laurelle's breath catches, and I hold still. Reaching underneath my cock, I push a finger into her wet pussy. It eagerly sucks me in, and Laurelle moans.

"Full, Emrys. I'm so full of you," she cries.

I retreat my hips and finger before entering both her holes again at the same time. Fucking her ass with shallow thrusts, I take some of her sweet come and begin to rub her clit. Her hips push back to meet my thrusts as her moans become incoherent.

"Emrys, I'm coming!"

Her ass tightens, and I slip my fingers back inside her pussy. Her greedy cunt clamps around my fingers as her come soaks my hand. Looking over her shoulder, her face is a picture of euphoric bliss, and it takes me over the edge. To know I'm the one who brought this pleasure to her is a privilege.

It's too fast, but I can't bring myself to care.

My seed spills into her tight ass as I gently fuck it into her. She moans softly as her muscles loosen once more. The last spray of seed leaves me, and I pull out of her tight body. I pull her cheeks apart and watch my seed leak from her ass and trail down her pretty slit. The sticky come gathers at her entrance before dripping onto the bed below.

I gently smack her ass before nipping it gently. Laurelle yelps before breaking off into a fit of giggles. She slumps forward on the bed, but not before capturing my hand and pulling me down beside her.

Curling her spine against my chest, our hands hold each other between her breasts. I turn and inhale her scent, loving the way her soft hair sticks to my sweaty skin. With a deep sigh, her ass presses against my cock, and it rises to life once more.

Laurelle's yawn quickly dispels any notion of another round.

"You have to be tired now," she murmurs. "I could sleep for a week."

I nod against her shoulder. My soul mingles with hers as I hold her. The two of us become one after the intensity of our coupling. I've never felt this way. The satisfaction I felt with previous loves is nowhere near what I feel right now.

I've had her in every way I can. I'll keep her and pleasure her and love her. Love.

It blasts through me, overwhelming all my senses. I've known that I've loved her from the moment she landed in my realm.

Why have I not told her? I should've told her every moment we've been together. She wants to stay with me. Surely I've done enough to earn hers? Maybe she's just waiting for my confession before surrendering her own.

Possessiveness—needing to lay this ultimate claim— burns my blood as I tighten my hold on her.

"I love you, my blossom," I say.

Her response never comes and as I glance down at her face I know why. She's out cold. Her breath is deep and even.

A small smile curls my lips as I wave my hand and the silk sheet covers us. I'll tell her again in the morning. After all, we have eternity together. Laurelle is mine. I've claimed her just as she's claimed me. For the first time, the future doesn't seem so much like an unending chore. It's filled with hope, excitement, and love.

My eyes grow heavy and it's not long before I'm following Laurelle into a deep restful sleep.

LAURELLE

Golden sunlight streams into my eyes.

Shifting slightly, my muscles protest the movement. Despite the soreness of my muscles and between my legs, I'd gladly forgo my discomfort in order to relive last night a thousand times. All of it had been wonderful. A wonderful, wild dream.

No not a dream—a real-life fantasy.

The muscular arm draping across my waist tethers me to this bed and my body. A firm reminder that everything that's happened since I stepped foot in this faerie realm is very real. My life began last night and every day will be just like these past two days. Perfect, magical, and filled with so much love it pours from me.

Emrys has done more than enough to earn my love. When he wakes I shall tell him.

Licking over my lips, I'm pleased to still have the taste of my king there. I want more of him. Forever will not be enough. He's made good on his word and has freed me from my old life. Now instead of shame, all I feel is freedom flowing through me. Unbridled lust and desire dance in my blood and demand I give into it with Emrys.

I have to get a look at him.

Rolling onto my other side, I stare up at his handsome face. Relaxed in sleep, he looks younger. His chest moves with each deep breath. Taking my hand, I gently trace my finger over his cheeks and along his strong jaw.

He inhales sharply, and his dark eyes blink open. His hand captures mine against his chin and brings it to his lips. His mouth lays kisses along the pulse at my wrist before giving it a gentle bite. I sigh and shift closer to him.

"You made good on your word," he grumbles. "We've been sleeping in here near a week."

I gasp and pull back to look at him. His green lips curl into a smirk.

"In human time, of course. In the meadow, it's only been a few hours."

I smile and shake my head, delighting in the warmth of his naked skin against mine.

"Some beast ravaged me well into the morning. I was in dire need of my beauty sleep."

"Some beast?" He raises a white brow.

I give a prim nod. In a flash, Emrys rolls me onto my back. His body slides between my splayed thighs. His hands circle my wrists and bring them above my head. The silk sheets and pillows cushion my body and bring me even closer to his.

"If I remember correctly, it was you—naughty girl—who begged this beast to fuck your ass."

I gasp schooling my features into a picture of mock outrage.

"A lady would never do such a thing."

Emrys chuckles before joining his mouth with mine. The kiss is gentle, and tender, in a way that brings tears to my eyes. I don't let them fall, I only kiss him harder. Everything is perfect. An old insecurity worms it's way into my heart. Is all of this too good to be true? Am I worthy of such a picturesque life?

Emrys breaks me from my thoughts as his lips tickle my ear.

"I see no lady here, only a queen. Queens demand whatever they please."

My hands cup his head as my eyes lower. I can't stop the words from passing through my lips. I hate this insecurity I still carry. Will it leave me with time? Or is this one last gift from my parents I'll never be able to rid myself of?

"Are you so certain of me? Of our connection to have bound me to you in such a way?"

Emrys pulls back, his brows lowering over his dark eyes.

"Are you having doubts?" he asks. His claws cup my cheek and force my gaze to meet his.

Biting my lip, I shake my head. Who can I share my worries with if not him? After all, he is the only one who can truly eradicate them for me.

"Just old insecurities threatening to ruin everything. I never felt good enough during my old life. I just worry that you've made a mistake. I'm sorry, I shouldn't doubt you. After all that you've done for me."

Shame, an ugly and all too familiar emotion makes my eyes lower.

"Never apologize for your feelings," he growls. "It will take time for you to unlearn the lies taught to you in the human world."

I shake my head in agreement. Emrys tightens his hold on me, and I feel his hard cock rub against my wet pussy. I let out a soft moan as he does it again, my desire replacing any other feelings. My eyes snap up to his.

"As for your insecurities..." His tongue licks over the shell of my ear. "I'll fuck them out of you. Your place is beside me. Or better yet, my place is inside of you for eternity."

I smile and lift my hips. His cock nudges my entrance as I meet his heated gaze.

"Then that's what you shall have."

Our chests speed up as we stare at each other, the desire and love we shared last night raging inside us again. Demanding we claim each other and bring the threads of souls together once more. The heat of bodies burns away all doubts.

Love. I must tell him. Now, I won't keep this to myself any longer.

"Emrys," I say. My hands tangle in his hair. "I—"

Unease curdles my stomach. Something is wrong. I can feel it. The meadow dims, and the breeze whips through the open window. It's cold and stings my nose with its metallic scent. Emrys roars, his chest vibrating against mine as he sits straight up in the bed.

"Intruders," he spits. His dark eyes glow with a fury I've never seen before. "I'll deal with them at once, my blossom."

I pull the silk sheet to my chest as I watch Emrys tear the room apart. He yanks on his thin, dark-colored pants. With a wave of his hand, an unbuttoned white shirt covers his back and flows down his arms. Anger pours from him as I watch his crown grow—the branches becoming thicker and the leaves denser.

Whoever made the mistake of interrupting us will feel the full wrath of my king.

"You will be safe here, my blossom. I'll be back to fill your needy little pussy in no time. You have my word."

My cheeks heat as Emrys heads towards *The Great Oak's* opening. Somehow, I manage to find my voice.

"Wait," I say. Emrys turns towards me, his fury melting into affection the longer he stares at me. "I am the queen now. Perhaps we should see to these trespassers together."

My hand gently touches the flower crown. The petals weave between my curls and dance under my fingers as if they are eager for my touch. This is my life now, and I want to claim it. My role here is important; while I love sharing Emrys's bed, I want to have a larger purpose than just a lover.

I want the responsibility of caring for the land and the people who set me free. Ruling over them with my king at my side is a privilege. I won't shrink from my duties.

Emrys pads over to me. His hand meets mine in my hair and gently traces over the petals of the wildflowers. It sends a shiver down my spine as I feel them revel in his attention.

"My beautiful, fierce queen. You would do me this honor of ruling by my side?"

"Always," I say. Emotion clogs my throat as he helps me from the bed.

He growls at my exposed body, the remnants of his seed still clinging to my chest and between my legs. With a wave of a hand, they are washed away, and I feel like I've just bathed in the warmest bath.

"You have *The Great Oak's* magic now, my blossom. Use it," Emrys encourages.

I stare down at my body and concentrate. Light flows from my chest as I reach inside myself, where Emrys and I are tied together. Power tingles at my fingertips as the scent of fresh flowers coats the air. Closing my eyes, I concentrate on what I want to appear.

Gasping, I feel something soft cover my body. I open my eyes to watch flowing white fabric decorated with light blue and purple flowers cover my body. The skirt is long, as are the sheer sleeves, but the neckline is low enough to enhance the swells of my breasts.

My feet remain blissfully bare.

"Perfect. You're too beautiful for any realm," Emrys states, grabbing my hand.

Leaning into his side, I press up on my toes and peck him on the lips.

"You make me feel beautiful. Powerful, too."

"As any good king should."

"How much power did you give me—or rather *The Great Oak*?"

His smile turns salacious as we pass through the trunk's opening. The cool morning air tickles my cheeks. The sharp metallic scent is still there. The wind guides us back towards the clearing where, no doubt, the intruders are being kept.

As an intruder myself, perhaps I'll show them mercy. Maybe their happiness resides down here as well.

"*The Great Oak* gave you a taste of the depth of your power. If you want more, all you have to do is ask. Or better yet—"

Emrys pulls me against his side and dives his tongue into my mouth. He kisses me thoroughly, tasting me until I forget where I am or where we are going.

"I can just fuck more of my power into you. How does that sound?"

"Delicious," I moan. He kisses me firmly once more before taking my hand again as we walk towards the meadow. "You make everything so easy for me."

"Nothing is more precious to me than you. If you wanted my crown, I'd cleave it from my head just to see you smile."

"Ugh," I wrinkle my nose at that gory image. I give his hand a squeeze. "That's sweet, but I prefer your head fully intact."

"As you wish, my blossom."

The closer we get to the meadow, the more Emrys's posture stiffens. Magic swirls around him on an invisible breeze. He glows with menace. The picture of destructive power, I almost expect the trees to tremble in his wake. Indeed, some of the sprites do as we pass. Their bodies dim as they hide under passing branches.

Emrys is every bit the terrifying king, but to me, he could only be my sweet lover.

Lover. The word doesn't sound right for what he is to me. It seems too fleeting. Yet, we've given no vows—there's been no discussion of what we are only that we belong to each other. Is that enough? Do I require such a pathetic human title from a creature with unlimited power?

My steps slow, and Emrys turns towards me. Concern is written on his face. Before he can ask me what's wrong, my worries slip from my lips. Damn my parents for poisoning me with such fickle insecurities.

"Are we married?" I blurt out. Emrys merely blinks at me. "I mean—will we be married? Is that something your kind does?"

The silent stretches for a moment I curse my errant tongue. Why did I have to make this awkward? He's made me his queen—what does it matter if I'm his wife or not? I should be grateful enough for this.

Emrys pinches my chin and holds my stare.

"I own you in every way. Just as you own me." I lick over my dry lips. "Is marriage important to you, my blossom?"

"It's so trivial, I know. It's just—"

"Nothing you want is trivial. Now, start again."

My body relaxes. I should've known he'd understand. No longer do I have to apologize for my feelings or feel burdened by them. My feelings are normal—natural. What's unnatural is disregarding them in order to appease someone else. I did so for my father and was preparing to do so for my future husband.

No more. I will never apologize for what I want again.

"Marriage is important to me. I want us to be united in that way."

Emrys nods, a small smile on his lip.

"Then, as king of this realm, I pronounce us married. Our subjects as our witnesses."

Raising his hand, I watch as he pinches the air and brings his fingers in front of my face. There, sitting between his thumb and forefinger is a delicate gold band decorated with a series of colored gemstones. It sparkles in the bright sun. My hand trembles as he takes it in his own.

"You are my everything. Wife, queen, lover. The other half of my soul," he says, sliding the ring onto my finger. It's a perfect fit. Tears rush to my eyes. "You are my heart. My mate. The one I took into *The Great Oak* to fulfill the prophecy. You are the only thing that truly matters to me."

"Quite romantic, husband." My giggle is watery. Emrys presses his lips to my forehead as the sprites around us cheer. Tucking my hand in his again, I admire my new ring as we walk the last few steps into the meadow's clearing.

The ring is perfect—just like everything else here. Nothing could ruin life here.

Until I see the humans clustered in the center of the meadow.

My stomach clenches, and my head feels strange.

There's a handful of men, all dressed in the regalia of royal guards. Bile rises in my throat as I take in their discarded banner. It's the royal seal of Prince Carysen's family.

The breath is ripped from my lungs as I fully take in the scene. A pair of royal guards are swinging their sharp swords at a swarm of faeries. Their bodies are barely two feet tall, yet they have these grown men shaking with fear. I might have found the whole thing funny if I wasn't so shocked.

Especially as I watch the three sisters bang against the guards' helmets, causing them to stumble.

My heart twists as I see the pathetic figure cowering behind the four royal guards. Prince Carysen—my intended —covers his ears as a handful of sprites pull at his sandy brown hair. He waves a gloved hand at them. His clothes are gaudy, yet clearly, they are showing signs of the fall he took to get down here. Grass stains mar the silk of his overcoat, and mud is caked on the fingers of his riding gloves.

His eyes finally open and meet mine. The cruelty there steals my breath, and I take a step back. Emrys is immediately at my side.

"My blossom, what's wrong?"

I open my mouth to answer, my eyes whipping between him and the prince. I don't get a chance to explain before a voice dripping in condemnation rips through the meadow.

"There she is," calls Prince Carysen, pushing from between his guards. "Of course, *you'd* manage to end up in a place like this."

He pays for that little show of courage when a pair of female faeries hiss at him, swiping at his pants with their claws. The guards manage to shove them back. Both the sprites and faeries retreat even as their muscles stay coiled.

I can feel their anger as if it is my own. It hums through

me, as does the unease of these latest arrivals. They don't belong here—they can't stay. If Emrys feels it too, he makes no indication as he gathers me to his side, and we face the wrath of my betrothed.

"What a great fucking mess this," Prince Carysen exclaims. "A month at least, we've been searching for you. A month without the dowry I was counting on your father providing me."

Emrys's grip on me tightens, his rage hot against my side.

Prince Carysen tracks the movement. His sneer misses nothing as the king holds me, our connection clear—especially as his ring glows on my finger.

"Why am I not surprised to find you here? Whoring yourself out to these foul creatures. No doubt you've let them take turns with you. How ashamed your family will be when they learn what's become of you."

One of the sisters—Pond—buzzes in front of his face and uses her hand to smack him in the eye. He howls and doubles over. Despite his cruel words, I can't help my smile at watching him in pain.

"You fucking bitch!" he roars. Whether it's at me or Pond, I'm not sure.

Wiping at his eyes, they blaze with blue fury.

"You could've just married me. Let me put some heirs in your belly and be done with it. Now, we're trapped in this fucking forsaken land with a bunch of—"

"Enough."

Emrys's voice cuts through the clearing with authority. Even the breeze stops blowing.

His claw skims up my back until he reaches my tense shoulders. Gently, he pulls them down and uncoils me. I hadn't even realized how much Carysen's words affected me until Emrys helps me right myself. Each vile word made me turn inwards, and the wrath on Emrys's face tells me they won't go unpunished.

Tracing a claw over my cheek, I let his power flow into me. I won't hide, and I won't cower. I belong only to Emrys, and he will keep me safe from monsters like Carysen.

My king turns his dark eyes onto my former betrothed, and I watch him and his guards pale.

"How dare you insult my queen." His voice cuts through the clearing like a knife. "You hurl those disgusting words against the woman I love. Saying she is no more than breeding stock and a few bits of gold. She is worth more than any coin. Any jewel. She is worth more than life."

A shiver of pleasure sings down my spine at his declaration.

With a wave of his claws, the trees around us shake before becoming a riot of snapping twigs and cracking branches. Invisible hands rip the swords from the guards' hands. Defenseless, they can do nothing as those mighty oak trees reach with their sentient branches and wrap them around their arms and legs. They scream as they are hoisted into the sky. Bucking against their wooden shackles, their fight is futile.

Carysen's eyes are wide as his fine clothes tear against the branches. He thrashes the most, tears streaming down his ruddy cheeks. Pain and fear dance in his eyes. How many women have felt the same in his presence? All of those former betrothals ending in their disappearances— his sister confirmed to me what happened.

He deserves every moment of this pain.

"Now you will die for your insults," Emrys commands.

Like whips, branches wrap around their throats and hoist them further into the sky. They thrash and gargle.

Carysen's satin gloves rip against the branch as he tries to dislodge it from around his neck.

For so long, I have been afraid of men like him—of my father and his expectations held up by my mother. Their rigid ideals stole so much from me, and I won't allow them to take anymore. Why should I hide in front of a coward like Carysen? A vermin who soaks the front of his trousers like a scared little boy.

My shoulders straighten as I feel the power of this realm —of Emrys and *The Great Oak*—flow through me.

"Wait," I command and watch as the trees listen. They stop tightening for a moment.

Emrys turns to me and awaits my command. I smile at him and let my love for him show. He loves me. He told Carysen—told his whole realm. I'll show him the same devotion in a moment. Right now, I have something important to tell this sniveling prince.

Taking a step forward, I level my gaze at Carysen and let cruelty flood my gaze.

"My father forced me to marry you in order to gain power. Power I never would've benefitted from. He did the same with my other siblings, shackling them all to their own loveless unions." I take another step as snot leaks from Craysen's red nose. Petulant child. "You would've been cruel to me. Your own sister clued me into the depths of your depravity and, with courage—something you could never be accused of having—helped me escape you."

"Laurelle, please, let me—"

"Silence." My voice echoes around the clearing, strong and unwavering. "Here I am safe—important. I have power and get to decide what I am. I have my freedom. My desires are many and indulged in. You may call me a whore, but that word means nothing coming from a monster like you."

"Please," Caysen chokes.

I merely incline my head, and the branch wraps tighter around his throat. Glancing behind me, I meet Emrys's gaze. It's just the same as it always is. Gentle and loving, clearly, he enjoys me reclaiming my power. His cock presses firmly against the front of his pants. I lick my lips.

Soon.

Turning back towards my prey, I grin.

"Do you know what true power is?" Carysen shakes his head as much as he can. "It's knowing that you'll be a forgotten human prince. It's knowing that I will live here powerful, free, and eternal. And more than anything, It's knowing that this creature, as you've called him, will kill you in an instant. He only waits for my command because he loves me."

I glance over my shoulder and meet Emrys's dark eyes as I say clearly, "Just as I love him."

Emrys growls, taking a step towards me, but I have one final edict as queen to deliver to our prisoner.

"Or he'll let me kill you, and I'll live in peace knowing you can never harm another person. And as much as I would love to be the one who ends you." I feel Emrys at my back as I smirk at Carysen. "I need to give my husband a wedding present. My love, would you please kill this pathetic man? I need you inside of me again."

Carysen babbles out a plea, but I'm already turning towards my faerie king. He smiles down at me as I wrap my hands around his neck and press our bodies together.

"With pleasure."

The branches snap together with a wave of his claws. I don't even watch as I hear the life being choked from Carysen and his guards. The cheers of our loyal subjects swallow up their last breaths. Their deaths aren't worth my note—Carysen's legacy has already been erased.

"Take their bodies away," I command my king.

The branches twist, and I hear a whipping through the air. In a moment, a distant thud can be heard just beyond the meadow. Let them be eaten by the wildlife here as their final act in this world.

My hands go to the back lacings of my gown and I undo them. Emrys's eyes heat as he watches me. Sliding the dress off my body, I hear the tittering of sprites and faeries all around us. Let them watch. I need my king.

He growls as I take his hand and place it on my breast.

"Now fuck me," I command him.

His mouth lands on mine as he gives my breast a squeeze. I'm flattened to the damp grass below us, and his tongue tangles with mine. Palming my breast, he quickly cups the other as I raise my hips, desperate to get some much-needed friction there.

The sprites and faeries cheer for us—whispering praise in our ears as they fly overhead. I can hear a few tinkling moans, and I know they're overcome just like their queen and king.

My hands rip off Emrys's white shirt before going to the tie of his pants. His teeth sink into my neck as I moan and rub my wet pussy against the bulge in his pants. His tongue skims up his bite as I thrash in his grasp. I'm soaking and desperate.

"You've bloomed, my blossom. Powerful and free. The real you is a sight to behold."

His mouth meets mine, and I moan into our kiss.

"You freed me. I'm never going back to who I was again. I can't. Not now, not ever."

He groans against me, and suddenly, his pants are off.

His massive cock bobs between our bodies, the tip already leaking with delicious seed. Before I can wiggle down to taste him, he grips his length in his hand and lines it up with my entrance. Lifting my hips with his free hand, he sheaths himself inside me in one strong thrust.

My muscles are still sore, but I accommodate him nonetheless. I love the burn of him inside of me. I crave it more than anything. Pressing up on my heels, he grips my hips and jerks me forward onto his length. We work in tandem to heighten each other's pleasure. It's so deep this way, our movement frantic with lust.

His eyes heat my blood. My breasts bounce with the force of each thrust, and I know my body is hurtling towards its peak. Fire licks up me, and I can't wait to erupt.

"Watching you order their deaths made me harder than I've ever been," Emrys growls.

"Does a cruel queen make you hard?" I ask.

"You make me hard." He impales me on his length as I let out a loud moan. "I should've known you enjoyed being watched."

My eyes take in the crowd around us. The air is thick with lust and couplings. Their beady eyes watch Emrys take me in this primal way—their mouths fall open as they glow brighter. A smile curls my lips as I turn back towards my king.

"Does that make me a naughty girl?" The question is as coy as I can manage while he fucks me with renewed vigor.

"Yes," he growls. "Next, you'll ask me to share you."

"Never," I say softly. His thrusts falter, but I pump my hips in time. My climax is swiftly approaching.

"Never?"

"Unless you wish to share me?"

"No," he growls.

"That's what I thought." I smile. "I don't want to share you either. They can watch, but nothing more. You're only for me."

"Posessive for a lady."

"A lady who knows exactly what she wants."

Lifting up on my elbows, I push my chest up and wrap my arms around Emrys's neck. He leans back and pulls me with him. His length is still deep inside of me as I balance on his lap. Working my hips, I grind down on his length over and over. The force of this position has my teeth smacking together.

I need more. I need it deeper than before.

With a shove, Emrys lands flat on his back. Balancing my hands on his chest, I raise my hips and lower myself on his massive cock. At this angle, my clit brushes against the base of his cock. My knees sink into the soft ground as I slam down on him over and over again.

Breasts bouncing, Emrys grips one in his claw and snarls. Raising his hips to meet mine, his cock hits my womb, and my eyes roll back in my head. I ride him for all that I'm worth. My muscles feel like jelly, but I keep going, my climax already tightening my stomach.

Our subjects encourage us, and that only adds to my pleasure.

"A queen this wanton is perfect for our king," one whispers. "Look at that ring!"

"She takes him so well. Should we really be watching?" another asks.

"Of course we should!" replies a tinkling voice. "Now get over here, and we can do our own fucking."

A giggle bursts from me as my nails embed in Emrys's chest. My curls cling to my back as I toss my head back and let my king take over. He holds my hips and lowers me onto his length. My pleasure steals my thoughts, but my mouth manages to move.

"This is what I've always wanted. When I would dream of my future, this is what I desired."

"Participating in a faerie orgy?" Emrys quips. His brows are lowered in concentration.

Despite my impending orgasm, I can't help but laugh.

"To feel like this. To be loved and to be in love." My mouth lowers to his, and I kiss him, pouring my soul into it. "You made a dream I hadn't even remembered I dreamed come true."

His hands wrap around my back and lock me to him. Raising up, he powers into me from below. My clit drags back and forth against him, and it's all I need. I scream into his mouth as my body explodes.

Muscles tighten and strain as bliss coats my body. I shake through it all, soaking Emrys until his body jerks below me, and he floods me with his seed.

"Laurelle." He fucks his come into me as it squelches between us to soak the grass. His warmth ties our souls together as he places soft kisses against my lips.

Peeling my eyes open, I notice the wildflowers that have grown around us. My smile is small as I meet my king's stare. His hands skim up my back and tangle in my hair. Bringing our faces close together, I let him see the truth in my gaze. I let him glimpse the soul that he owns.

"I love you, my king."

"I love you, my blossom," he answers.

Sinking onto his chest, my head turns out towards the meadow. The sun is high in the sky and illuminates the nearly empty clearing. All traces of our intruders are gone. There's just calm, serene peace. Clearly, our subjects found their peaks at the same time we did.

It's absolutely perfect.

"What would you like to do on your first official day as queen?"

Emrys's voice pulls me from my daze. Turning, I rest my chin on his chest. His smile is full of love as he curls a lock of my hair around his finger. The birds caw over my head, and I bite my lip at the idea that hits me.

"There is one thing," I say, crawling up his chest and pressing a kiss to his lips.

"Name it."

Nuzzling under his chin, I let out a content sigh.

"Is there any way you can make me fly?"

EPILOGUE - EMRYS

Many, Many Faerie Years Later

"Have we ever made it through one of these parties without you ruining my dress?"

Laurelle's question ends in a gasp as I rip open the front of her green silk gown. Instantly, her luscious breasts spill free, and my mouth comes down to claim a hard nipple. They taste sweet—just like every part of her does.

The lively music and smell of fire swirl around us as I see to my queen in this empty corner at the edge of the meadow. Usually, my queen likes a more public display, but tonight, I need some time alone with her in the dark.

"Are you asking me to stop?" I nip the fleshy swell of her left breast before sucking her right nipple into my mouth.

"Never," she moans.

Her hunger for me—just like her delicious wantonness —has only grown over the years we've spent together. She looks like same. Beautiful as ever. More so now as she glows with more golden power with each passing year.

The time we've spent together feels short in comparison to those dark, lonely years I was without her. How much time has passed in the human world? Sixty years? Seventy? Who knows. My blossom hasn't aged a day—her life is as eternal as mine. Even more so now that we regularly venture into the heart of *The Great Oak* to renew its power.

We are two willing and diligent subjects in that regard.

"We should be entertaining them. They are our guests, after all."

Laurelle's half-hearted protests are whispered against my lips as my tongue dives back in to dance with hers. *Great Oak*, she is sweet. Sweeter with time and familiarity. I've memorized her a thousand times—could tell you the number and shape of every freckle on her gorgeous body—and yet when my lips find hers, I am just as overwhelmed as if it was our first kiss.

I won't deny my pleasure nor hers for the sake of some arrivals.

"Guests that don't need us at the present moment," I growl, my claws squeezing her breasts.

"Still." She tries to argue against my mouth even as I feel her small hands go to the tie of my pants. "It seems rude. They came all this way as a show of good faith."

Kissing my queen once more, I press my forehead to hers.

"We had one of these more than a century ago, and it was a boring and dull affair," I state. Raising a dark brow, disbelief is written all over her lovely face. "I'll concede that this time is a bit more...interesting."

Laurelle giggles. "You can say that again. They're no better than us."

Glancing over my shoulder, my blossom is, as always, correct.

I spy our guests and their mates. How interesting it is that creatures of our ilk each claimed our own human beauties. Though none of them are as gorgeous as my Laurelle, no one ever will be. Still, the delicate females are in sharp contrast to their male counterparts.

The first pair I spot is the demon Asgorath with his dark-haired human, Irys, in his lap. Golden goblets of faerie wine lay discarded at their feet. He's treated us to his demon form this evening. His skull burns with a red-hot fire that matches the blushing cheeks of his pale human lover. Together, their hands work each other through their clothing.

His hand skates under her thin black dress, and his long tongue caresses the side of her neck. Her moan echoes around the meadow as her hand curls into his dark cloak.

"I've kept you to myself for too long, little one. Shall we show them how wet your pretty pussy still gets for me after all these years?" the demon growls. His hand pumps between her legs as his other peels her long skirt higher.

"Yes, please," she whimpers.

A small smile plays on my lips as I turn to my old aquatic friend. His reign has been almost as long as mine and the demon's. He was always the most miserable amongst us, but that male is long gone. Especially as his eyes stare up at his crimson-haired human, Melody, they are just as entangled in each other as the demon and his mate are.

Albeit a bit more so due to Zalenyk's tentacles. His semi-human form is long gone, and now he is merely a slimy mass of muscles and slithering appendages. Hosting her up by her arms, his tentacles slide underneath her skirt as her eyes roll back in her head. She lets out a keening sound when a second one disappears between her thighs.

"Wet for me, sweet one. Beg for me to fuck you in front of everyone," the Kraken commands.

Melody's eyes blaze with icy fire.

"Make me," she challenges.

The Kraken shakes with dark laughter as a third tentacle hoists up her skirt. His other limbs wrap around her and bring her into his massive body, swallowing her high-pitched moans.

Lastly, there is the dragon—the youngest among us with the most unfortunate backstory. However, there is no sign of the cursed male, as he and his golden-haired, Anwyn, are a lot farther along than the other couples.

He's already drug her behind a small rose bush. His green-scaled wings thrust towards the night sky while Anwyn's bare legs dangle from his powerful hips. Her blue dress is left forgotten on their shared chair, along with their food.

His tail slides towards her until she lets out a deep sigh. Wings flexing, I watch his hips jerk forward and earn a rewarding moan from his human.

"This is what you get, my treasure. Take your punishment for almost allowing them a glimpse of my precious little cunt," the dragon growls.

"Lassar, you fill me so good. You own my pussy, no one else will see it. Never," she mewls.

I watch her hands sink into his strong backside as their moans join the cacophony of the other couples. Laurelle's and I's will mingle with theirs soon.

Turning my attention back to my own treasure, she smiles up at me, and my heart stumbles in my chest. Gripping the tatters of her dress, I pull it from her as the primal part of me demands we claim her just as the others are. To show that this beautiful female is our mate and no one else will get the pleasure of her flesh.

This meeting, though momentarily paused, is an important one. It was called to establish our boundaries. While I reign over *The Woods* creator—*The Great Oak*—the realm it sprouted above has been left unruled. It hasn't been a problem in centuries yet, but our arrivals made sure to tell me of the new creatures that have begun to call it home.

Some linger on the outskirts and the undiscovered portions of the dense forest, while each monster here today has laid claim to a different section. A portion of The Woods will be Asgortah's domains, where unlucky souls can still seek out bargains. Lassar will take the cave system and hoard treasure as he sees fit. Zalenyk will control the waterways in and around *The Woods* while I will remain here.

Securing my realm as I always have and always will with my queen by my side.

Zalenyk and Lassar have been very territorial lately due to their families continuing to grow. Both of their unions have brought forth a new species of half-human, half-creature, and their domains' safety is paramount. Whatever the future has in store for these new halfling children, we can all rest easy knowing we are in support of keeping them safe.

Looking down at my lovely queen, maybe one day, the two of us will embark on that adventure together when the time is right. For now, I am far too greedy to share her and will continue to bring her the contraceptive herbs each morning.

Her gown falls to the floor as I pin her to the nearest tree. The smooth skin of her thighs wraps around me, and her skin glows like a star in the moonlight. Entering her in one swift thrust, I weave my fingers through her curls to cup her head. Her breasts bounce with the impact of each thrust as her moans echo around us.

"Still so tight, my blossom. Your perfect cunt is too much," I groan.

"It welcomes my king whenever he wants it. You rule it just as you do my heart."

The primal surge to claim her harder rips from me as I yank her from the trunk of the tree and lay her on the soft grass. The sprites gather around us and buzz on their colorful wings. Faeries gather, too, their short bodies watching with dark eyes as I take their queen. Grunts and moans soon drown out the sound of the music as everyone in the meadow swiftly gives in to the lust permeating the air.

My realm sparkles. *The Great Oak* is pleased with the number of couplings occurring and is flooding it with primal magic.

Yet my eyes remain on my beauty. Her cheeks are flushed, and her eyes are wide as I spear into her wet flesh once more. Her legs go up on my shoulders as I hold her hips in my hands. Fucking her onto my length, I revel in the sloppy sounds her wet pussy makes as I take her hard and fast in the damp grass.

"It's perfect," she moans. "Every bit of this life with you is better than any dream."

"You're my only dream," I growl, increasing my tempo as I feel her muscles start to clench down on me. "My only desire. There is nothing beyond you. Beyond this."

"I love you, Emrys," she sighs, her hands curling into the grass beside her.

"I love you," I echo and slam into her with a force that has her body sliding along the wet ground.

Her body thrashes in my grip, but I don't stop. The wave of her pleasure is just about to crash. When it does, her pussy strangles my hard cock, and her back arches. Her mouth is open in a silent scream as I let myself go. My spine locks, and I flood her little pussy with my seed and fuck it into her so she gets every drop. It pools between us before hitting the grass below. She eagerly welcomes every drop, rocking her hips forward to capture it all.

Once my body stops trembling, I pull her from the ground and hold her in my arms. My claws skim up her back as her own wrap around my neck. Our crowns tangle together just as the threads of our souls do.

She is mine. Always.

Much has changed over these years together, and change will only keep happening. With the new creatures stirring in *The Woods* and the future of these pairings and the children resulting from them still unclear, the only thing that's certain is that things will become different. I welcome it all, especially with Laurelle by my side.

The years without her were empty. Whatever these next ones bring will fulfill me in a way I never thought possible before her. Looking down at her face, I know she feels the same. As do the other monsters in my meadow. They said as much before the faerie wine really started to flow.

The power we've all wielded for so long was nothing without someone to share it with. Life without love— without our humans—isn't worth living. We will all do whatever we must to safeguard them and our futures together.

Rolling to my side, I tuck Laurelle against me. The cool evening breeze feels good against our hot skin that sticks together with our sweat. I peel one dark curl from her temple and wrap it around my finger.

Leaning down, I whisper all that I've just thought into her ear. I make promises of our future and more declarations of love than I can count. When her smile stretches so wide I'm sure her cheeks are beginning to ache, I kiss her perfect mouth and gaze into the soul I've claimed.

"You saved me. Fulfilling the prophecy saved my realm —my people—but you did more than that. I couldn't have survived another handful of centuries without you. Without this," I confess.

Her eyes sparkle with unshed tears as she kisses me back gently.

"You saved me too. From a life of cruelty, you've given me everything. You are everything to me."

The meadow around us glows as the sprites settle in, and the magic from our fucking flows through the land. I can't help my own smile as I take it all in. Things may be changing and yet my love for Laurelle will always remain.

I grin as my cock hardens against her hip. Gently, I take her shoulder and roll her onto her side with her back pressed up against my chest. My hand skims down her side, eliciting a high-pitched scream as she squirms. My ticklish little queen. I continue touching her until I reach her soft knee and lift it before settling her thigh along my hip.

Laurelle giggles and looks at me over her shoulder.

"What are you doing?" she asks.

I grin at her, showing the teeth I'll be biting her with in a moment. My claiming mark on her shoulder is starting to fade, and my blood demands I renew it.

"I haven't had your ass in a while."

Laurelle barks a laugh and shakes her head.

"You fucked me there this morning."

"See," I say, gripping my cock, still glossy from our releases, and pressing it against her back entrance. "That was a couple of days ago in the human realm."

"Instatiable beast," she murmurs. Her eyes glow with affection. "But you're mine. Eternally."

I thrust inside her tight ass, and she lets out a deep moan. Our souls sing as our connection is sealed once more. My blossom, my queen, my Laurelle. Perfection in every way. *The Great Oak* has blessed me beyond my wildest dreams.

"Eternally," I agree and thrust inside her again.

Princess Caryssa's story is coming...

ACKNOWLEDGMENTS

WOW! What started as just a writing exercise has now spawned into a four novella series with more on the way. I hope you loved Laurel & Emrys's story as much as I did writing it.

As always I want to thank my Beta Readers & ARC team! You guys provide such amazing insight and I couldn't get this book done without your help. Thank you to the amazing @hayaindesigns for my magnificent cover.

Lastly and most importantly, thank you to all of you! Without your guys love and support this series would've never gone to the places it did. Here's to more stories and getting lost in *The Woods*...

ABOUT THE AUTHOR

Charlotte Swan is a twenty-five-year-old, living in Chicago. When she is not dreaming about being whisked away to a world filled with magic and sexy monsters, she is busy being a freelance social media marketer and full-time smut lover. To read other series, hear about her upcoming projects, or to connect with her on social media please find her on her website or by scanning the code below.

www.authorcharlotteswan.com

ALSO BY CHARLOTTE SWAN

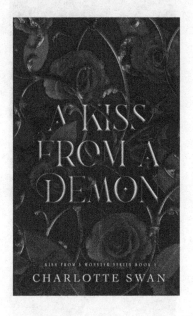

A Kiss From a Demon (Kiss From a Monster Series #1)

A Kiss From a Kraken (Kiss From a Monster Series #2)

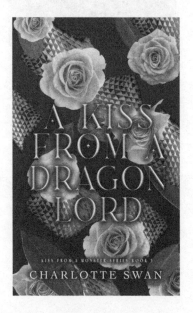

A Kiss From a Dragon Lord (Kiss From a Monster Series #3)

Taken by the Dark Elf King (Monstrous Mates Series #1)

Captured by the Orc General (Monstrous Mates Series #2)

Made in the USA
Monee, IL
23 September 2024